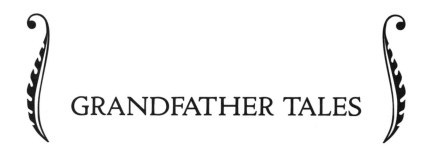

GRANDFATHER TALES

GRANDFATHER TALES

American-English folk tales selected and edited by
RICHARD CHASE; illustrated by BERKELEY WILLIAMS, Jr.

HOUGHTON MIFFLIN COMPANY

＊

To ALL THE GRANDFATHERS
and grandmothers who told while I listened;
and to Leonard, Eddie, Pat, Harold, Billy,
Dannie and Junior, David and Tommy,
Bobby, Gerald, Clinton, and Herbie —
all clean and ready for bed, who sat
around the big warm fireplace at
Small Boys' House one cold winter-time,
listening while I told;
and

＊

To ALL TELLERS AND LISTENERS
old and young, who discover what
Tom Hunt meant when he said,
"No, it'll not do just to read
the old tales out of a book.
You've got to tell 'em
to make 'em go right."

 # PREFACE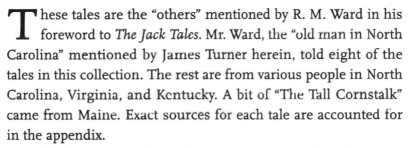

These tales are the "others" mentioned by R. M. Ward in his foreword to *The Jack Tales*. Mr. Ward, the "old man in North Carolina" mentioned by James Turner herein, told eight of the tales in this collection. The rest are from various people in North Carolina, Virginia, and Kentucky. A bit of "The Tall Cornstalk" came from Maine. Exact sources for each tale are accounted for in the appendix.

In this book I have taken a free hand in the re-telling. I have put each tale together from different versions, and from my own experience in telling them. I have told the tales to all kinds of listeners, old and young; and only then, after many tellings, written them down.

This spontaneous telling process is really important for you, too, the reader. After you have read these tales, put the book away and try telling one. You don't have to use dialect. Use your own common speech. Reading the printed word can never — especially for your young listeners — be the same as using the living word.

For me, the writing down of these tales has often been a difficult and tedious process. Mrs. Grover Long, a descendant of Council Harmon (through whose grandchildren *The Jack Tales* "and others" have been preserved), told me how she had once tried to put down "Old Counce's" tales on paper. "And I just couldn't do it," she said, "it all went stale on me."

Filling up blank sheets of paper is, indeed, not the same as the sound of your own voice shaping a tale as it wells up out of your memory and as your own fancy plays with all its twists and turns. And the best part of it is that finally by some mysterious process you find that you are listening to the tale yourself as much as the listeners around you. I'd really much rather *be telling* these tales to you instead of *having to sit here* all alone, pecking at a typewriter. It is not the same as hearing a hush settle down on a group of young people when a tale begins and watching their faces as they become more and more absorbed in what's going to happen next to little Jack, or to Mutsmag, or Wicked John, or Old Roaney. So, you try it! After you have learned the tales in silent print, shut the book and *"tell 'em."*

II

In getting the tales written down so I could re-tell them for you, the following people have been particularly helpful: Alice Cobb, James Taylor Adams and his wife, Dicy Roberts Adams, and their sons, Spencer and Simpson; John and Louise Powell; Berkeley Williams, Sr.; Charles and Ruth Seeger and Mike, Peggy, and Barbara; Miss Annie Willis; Robert A. Moore; Lois Fenn; Darwin and Barbara Lambert and Harvey, Priscilla, and Laura; James M. Hylton; George H. Tucker and his niece Carolyn Virginia Miller; and the following institutions: The Virginia Writers project (W.P.A.), Pine Mountain Settlement School, Berea College, Boone (N.C.) High School, Cove Creek School at Sugar Grove, North Carolina, Blue Ridge School at Saint George, Virginia, Stuart Robinson School, Huntsville (Ala.) Rotary Club, Charlottesville (Va.) Lions Club, Pittsburgh Authors' Club, University of Pittsburgh's Department of English, Madison College (Va.), Department of English at Western Reserve University — and many schools, little and large, in Virginia, where I have told tales.

R.C.

CONTENTS

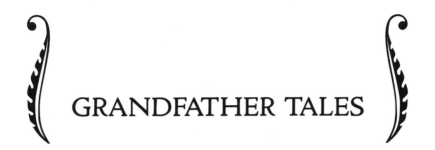

GRANDFATHER TALES

OLD-CHRISTMAS EVE

It was on one of my first trips to Crockett County that James Turner took me out to see Tom Hunt. Mr. Hunt lives alone in an old hewn-log house about a mile out of the county seat; and when James and I got out of the car that cold winter evening Tom was in the yard carrying logs of firewood toward the door. He threw us a hearty welcome and led the way in to the fire.

"How're ye doin'?" James asked as we stepped over the doorsill.

"'Bout like common, Jeems. They all well up at your place?" He laid the wood on the fire and poked glowing chunks underneath.

"We can eat all we can get!"

"Aaa Law!" Tom laughed back at him. "You'd 'a thought peace would 'a meant the end of hard times, now wouldn't ye?" He turned and faced us: a tall hardy old man of about fifty, gentle-featured, with iron-gray shock of hair, his eyes a bit shy as they glanced at me.

"Meet Dick Chase. He's in here huntin' up old songs and old tales."

1

Tom Hunt took my hand. "Proud to know ye. — Sit down, boys! Here, take these chairs. I'll fetch me one from the kitchen. Shuck off your coats and sit. You ain't in no hurry, are ye?"

We threw our coats on a big oak chest by the door, and the three of us pulled up to the flaming logs. The weather, the health of relatives and neighbors, local news, national news, world news, were duly discussed. A few queries were made as to where I was born and raised, then Tom asked, "Tales? What sort of tales you lookin' for? Old man Boyd, now, up on Dry Fork, he can tell ye everything he ever heard from the old folks back when he was a boy: all about when the Indians were in here, and the Battle of King's Mountain, and that other war — the one they fit over slavery."

"No, it's not history I'm lookin' for. It's tales about giants, and about a boy named Jack, and about the Devil comin' up here and gettin' — "

"Bobtail," Jeems broke in. "How he beat the Devil that time; and tales like 'Catskins,' and 'Poll and Betts and Mutsmag,' 'Old Dry Frye' — all that kind of foolishness."

"Oh, you want the old grandfather tales: 'Jack and Will and Tom,' 'Chunk o' Meat,' 'The Two Lost Babes' — them old impossibilities. Is that what you're after?"

"Exactly."

"Aaa Lord! That brings back old times. My granddaddy now, the one that built this house, he's taken me on his knee many a time, right there where you're a-sittin', and told me about Jack till my mother 'uld have to make him quit so I could go to bed. And my daddy and Uncle Kel Weaver could sit up and tell tales all night — and never tell the same tale twice!"

"Dick's done made a book out of all that about Jack: the way he learned it from an old man down in North Carolina."

"A book? Huh. — I saw one of the old tales in a book one of the Weaver kids brought by here the other day, Big Claus or somethin'. It was like 'Jack and His Heifer Hide' but it was so different from the way I knew it, it got me all bothered up. I got to thinkin' about that tale then, and next time one of them Weaver young 'uns asked me for it, why! it had got so cluttered up in my mind I told it end-over-backwards. I never could tell a tale unless I just told it straight out — unthoughtedly, you might say. — No, it'll not do: just to read the old tales out of a book. You got to *tell* 'em to make 'em go right."

Tom took the fire-shovel and with a sprinkling of ashes slowed down the heat that was blazing at our shins from the fresh flaming logs.

"Uncle Kel and Granny London — are they winterin' down here with the Weaver folks again?" asked Jeems.

"Came down the middle of November. Uncle Kel's just about quit farmin' now. — You know, that makes four generations at the Weaver house: Uncle Kel, Old Rob, Little Rob, and the two boys that are still at home."

Jeems rose. "Well, Tom, I expect we better be movin'. We'll come early next time and you and I will see what tales we can recollect for this man."

"Oh, no! You 'uns stay the night. Plenty of beds here. You've come at a good time, too. You know what date it is tomorrow?"

"January sixth," said Jeems.

"What else?" Tom asked pointedly.

"Old Christmas! Now that is so, ain't it! We ain't kept Old Christmas at my house since I was a kid, and I don't always remember it."

"Hit's not likely I'll forget it! All that Weaver gang keeps Old-Christmas Eve with me every year — ever since my wife died."

Tom took hold of the poker and pushed the forestick gently against the backlog. Bright yellow flames began to work along the front edge of the forestick. "Jeems," he said quietly, "Does this man know what Old Christmas is?"

"Twelfth night after Christmas Eve, Dick. That's tonight, the Eve of Old Christmas," explained Jeems.

"Now," said Tom, "there's a lot Old Kel and Granny can tell ye about old times, and the old music and all that. And we're liable to sit up all night carryin' on here. Aaa Lord! If it's the old tales ye want, boys, you better just stay a while. — Have ye eat?"

We had eaten at Jeems's place, but Tom took the large round-wick lamp out to the kitchen and made us join him. He brought out biscuits and butter, apple-butter, jellies, and canned fruit. A large pitcher of milk was carried in from the back porch; and finally a trivet held the percolator over hot coals on the hearthrock. While we ate, Jeems and Tom told me more about the Weaver family: Old Rob's fame as a tale-teller, and Granny's "delight in singin'." We had finished and just sat down by the fire again when a scuffling and stomping of feet on the porch announced the arrival of the generations of Weavers. Tom opened the door.

Old Kel, lanky and clean-shaven, grinned and cracked Tom a greeting as he navigated in on two stout hickory canes. Granny London's black eyes shot Jeems and me an inquisitive glance as she slipped a gray shawl from her narrow bent shoulders and moved toward the fire. Old Robin came booming in: neatly trimmed white hair and beard, apple-red cheeks, and gay blue eyes. He banged Jeems across the shoulders and wrung my hand like an old friend. "Welcome, stranger! Hit's good to see a new face once in a while. I been lookin' at these ugly folks here an awful long time!"

Delia, his stoutish wife, drawled, "Who ever told you you was such a pretty thing to look at?" as Tom helped her off with her coat. "Little" Robin (i.e., Robin Weaver, Jr.) proved as tall as Old Kel must have been before age struck him. He and his wife, Sarah, had about them the warm healthy look of those who work much in the outdoors.

They all knew Jeems. Tom brought me forward and made me known to them, as each took my hand with a "Proud-to-know-ye." Jeems and I retreated from the fireplace while they all milled about there warming, and the spell of formality and a stranger's presence was broken by Tom, asking, "Where's the boys?"

"Never you mind!" Old Rob shouted. "They'll be here directly."

"Old Kel's been puttin' 'em up to some foolishness or other," said Sarah.

"He's had Steve and Stan and a regular gang of young 'uns out there in the barn all week, a-practicin' on somethin' or other," said Delia, "and sech a racket and a hollerin' you never heard."

"Hit's that old dumb-show we used to do when I was a boy over beyond the Cumberland there — in Kaintucky," said Old Kel.

"What is it?" asked Jeems.

"You'll see soon enough!" — and Old Robin set chairs for Delia and Granny.

"Don't let on ye know a thing about it," warned Kel. "Hit really ought to be done without a soul knowin' it's comin' off."

Tom had fetched other chairs from about the house, but before we had all quite settled there was a scurry of children's feet and voices outside the door, a hush, then a timid knock.

"Come in!" Tom called. A big girl's face peered in at the door frame. "Come on in, Rhody."

Rhody entered, and a group of children stumbled over the sill behind her, wiggled out of coats, and squirmed out of sweaters. They mumbled a few good-evenin's, and after a brief hand-warming at the hearth scampered for seats: on Tom's big bed in the far corner, on the edge of the coat-laden chest by the door, on the floor by Granny's chair. The women reached out and hoisted three of the littlest ones up against their bosoms. One small boy leaned against Uncle Kel's knee. Two little girls struggled for the privilege of Old Robin's lap until he settled it by taking one on each knee.

"What you young 'uns expectin' to see?" Tom asked.

"That play-actin' the boys are fixin' to do," said Rhody. "Uncle Kel he told us about bringin' pennies, too."

"What play?" Old Robin burst out, with a most solemn face.

"No show here tonight! If ye wants to see a show you'll have to go to Newton to the movin' picture theater."

"No sech thing!" Rhody shot back at Old Rob. "They are, too, goin' to do that old dumb-show! We saw Steve and Stan goin' after the Sneed boys. We hid in the bresh till they got past us; and they both were all dressed up funny, and Steve was a-hollerin' some kind of crazy speech, and Stan told him to shut up till it was time to say it. — You can't fool us!"

This brought a burst of laughter from Rob and all the company. Tom sent two little boys for more wood. They struggled in with a big log which Jeems and Tom dropped in place on the fire. The two kids scurried back to their seats with suppressed giggles and quick glances toward the door. The room grew suddenly quiet. There was a creak and a quiet bump on the porch.

MUMMER'S PLAY

Outside in the gathering frosty dark a clear boy's voice began to sing. The other boys joined in, a bit unsteady at first, but the strong confident tones of their leader held them firm and kept the song going.

Joseph and the Angel

As Jo-seph was a-walking he heard an an-gel sing:
This night shall be the birth-night of Christ the Heav'nly
    King,
This night shall be the birth-night of Christ the Heavn'ly
    King.
He neither shall be born-ed in house nor in hall,
nor in a king's palace but in an oxen's stall.
He neither shall be washen in white wine nor red,
but in the clear spring water with which we were christen-ed.
He neither shall be cloth-ed in purple nor in pall,
but in the fair white linen that usen babies all.

JOSEPH AND THE ANGEL

As Jo-seph was a – walking

he heard an an – gel sing:

This night shall be the birth-night

of Christ the Heav'n-ly King,

This night shall be the birth-night

of Christ the Heav'nly King.

He neither shall be rock-ed in silver nor in gold, but in a
    wooden cradle that rocks upon the mold.
On the sixth day of January his birthday shall be,
when the stars and the mountains shall tremble with glee.
As Joseph was a-walking thus did the angel sing;
and Mary's son at midnight was born to be our King.

The song ended; and after a brief pause a loud knocking rattled the door, and a boy's voice shouted:

> *"Open the door and let us in!*
> *We come your favor for to win!*
> *We shall fight and we shall fall,*
> *and we shall try to please you all!"*

The boys by the chest dashed to open the door. A boy holding a broom and wearing an old battered Hallowe'en mask stepped in. He plunged into his next speech:

> *"We come here to wish you cheer!*
> *Money in your pockets all this year!*
> *I'm the presenter sent before,*
> *and with my broom I'll clear the floor.*
> *Room! Make room, and clear the way!*
> *Make some room to see our play!"*

The Presenter had worked his way to the center of the fireplace where he swept threateningly at us and we moved back to clear the view for all the company.

The rest of the actors had pushed just inside the door and stood huddled there. The Presenter having cleared the way, a boy in an old store-bought Santy Claus suit came forth. His hat and beard bore sprigs of holly.

"In comes I, Old Father Christmas,
hard times or not;
I know Old Father Christmas
will never be forgot."

Father Christmas strutted once around the "stage" and retired toward the door. Then out came a figure in a woman's long rumpled dress, with a paper-bag mask tied up into two horns, a cow's tail fastened on behind and a cowbell on each hip, a dead rabbit in one hand and a frying pan in the other.

"In comes I, Old Bet,
as ugly as can be;
and every man within this house
must now be kissed by me."

Old Bet pretended to try to kiss Tom and Old Rob who played up with a loud show of resistance. Bet retired and another masked boy came forth in an oversize coat, with stalks of wheat and mistletoe in his hat and a short club in his hand.

"In comes I, Old Barleycorn, the best in the land;
I'll fight and I'll fall, for the sake of you all."

The next boy wore a tall pointed cap down over his whole face, two holes cut for his eyes. Red paper streamers flowed from the peak of the cap. From under his coat a long flannel nightgown trailed down to his feet.

"In comes I, Mister Pickle Herring,
for to join this dance;
I had to wear grandma's nightdress
'cause I couldn't find my pants."

A boy with his face rouged all over, red nose, red ears, red neck, now mounted another boy who was wearing a horse's head made of two slabs of cardboard carton. The horse trotted forward with the red-faced one astride.

> *"I am the doctor pure and good*
> *and with my pills I'll stop the blood."*

The horse whinnied and kicked up a heel and took the doctor back to the door corner. Only one actor remained—a little horned devil with his face blackened. He had red and yellow streamers tied around neck, arms, and waist. He did not present himself— instead he rather tried to keep hidden behind the others. Now Old Bet and Barleycorn came forward together and the following dialogue took place with shouts and gestures:

> *"Old Barleycorn, the play's begun;*
> *we'll fry this hare and have some fun."*
> *"We'll beat it and whale it*
> *and cut it in slices,*
> *and take an old pot*
> *and boil it with spices."*
> *"We'll fry this hare!"*
> *"We'll boil it, I said!"*
> *"Fry it!"*
> *"Boil it!"*
> *"We'll fry it and no more be said;*
> *for if you dare to boil this hare,*
> *with my pan here I'll crack your head!"*
> *"My head's made of iron!*
> *My neck's made of steel!*
> *You can crack all you want,*
> *you can't make me feel!"*

"I'll cut your old coat full of holes
and make the buttons fly!"
"I'll cut you small as little flies
and use you up to cook mince pies!"
"I'll make your blood run cold as clay;
I'll fry YOU, and throw the hare away!"

Bet and Barleycorn went to it with club and frying pan. After a brief and noisy battle, Bet thrust her frying pan forward like a sword and gave a great slash at Barleycorn's middle, and Barleycorn fell prone before the fireplace.

All the actors chanted in unison:

"Now, Old Bet, see what you've done!
You've killed our own belov-ed one!"
"Horrible! Terrible! See what I've done!
I've cut him down like the evening sun!"

The actors all gathered about the corpse and wept and wailed, and then Bet shouted:

"Is there a doctor to be found
to cure this deep and deadly wound?
Is there a doctor near at hand
to heal him again and make him stand?"

The horse brought the Doctor at a fast gallop. The Doctor dismounted, and the weeping boys stood aside.

"Hold my horse, Pickle Herring."
"Will he kick?"
"No."
"Will he bite?"
"No."

"Take two to hold him?"

"No!"

"Hold him yourself then."

"What's that, you sassy rascal!"

"I got him, sir."

Pickle Herring took hold of the frayed rope that served the horse for a tail. Doctor and corpse and Old Bet now held the stage.

"What's your fee?"

"Eleven guineas, nine pounds, nineteen shillings, eleven pence, three farthings, six pecks of gingerbread for me, and six loaves of oats for my horse."

"That's too much."

"I'll throw off the gingerbread, and the oats."

At this the horse whinnied and kicked indignantly, but Pickle Herring finally gentled him down again by promising him a bale of water and a bucket of hay.

"What can you cure?"

> "The itch, the stitch, the stone, the bone,
> the young, the old, the hot, the cold,
> the measles, the wheezles, the spots, the gout,
> and if there's nineteen devils in I can bring twenty out."

"Here! Dose him out of this bottle."

"What's in it?"

> "Three quarts of nim-nam,
> one ounce of brains of a saw-horse,
> one pound of marrow out of a stool leg,
> one pint of pigeon's milk, strained through a side of sole leather,
> stewed in an old sow's horn, and stirred with a frog's feather."

"I'll hold up his head; you dose him."

The doctor raised Barleycorn's head and Bet plied the bottle. The corpse jumped up.

> *"Good morning to you all!*
> *A-sleeping I have been,*
> *and I've had such a sleep*
> *as the like was never seen;*
> *but now I am awake*
> *and alive unto this day;*
> *so we shall dance a little*
> *and end this play."*

The actors joined hands in a ring and wheeled once around with noisy buck-and-wing antics. Then they sprawled together in an all-pile-on tangle of legs and heads and arms. They began to extricate themselves, and above the merriment the voice of the little black devil rose from beside the door as he advanced on us with his broom.

> *"In comes I, Little Devil Doubt!*
> *If you don't give us money I'll sweep ye all out!*
> *Money we want, money we crave!*
> *If you don't throw us money,*
> *I'll sweep ye to your grave!"*

He swept vigorously toward Old Rob who backed away in mock alarm reaching in all his pockets for money, while all the kids shrieked and threw a shower of pennies at the little black devil. The boys, on all fours, rooted for pennies, and broke out in fresh scrambles as the grown-ups treated them with new showers of coins. Finally, the last penny was swept from where it had rolled under the bed, and the laughter subsided.

"You 'uns divide it up equal, now," said Old Kel. "That's the way we always done."

The mummers pooled their earnings in Old Bet's frying pan, and marched out singing:

> *"We are not London actors*
> *that act upon the stage,*
> *but we are country plowboys*
> *that work for little wage:*
>
> *Love and joy come to you,*
> *and to you a wassail too;*
> *and God bless you and send you a happy new year,*
> *and God send you a happy new year.*
>
> *Good master and good mistress,*
> *as you sit by the fire,*
> *remember us poor plowboys*
> *a-plowing in the mire:*
>
> *Love and joy come to you —"*

As we began re-settling ourselves, the boys came back in the door carrying masks and costumes which were piled on Tom's trunk by the far window. Tom led the Doctor and Devil Doubt out to the kitchen where they began removing rouge and burnt cork with much splashing and giggling. I had set my chair over by Granny and Uncle Kel.

"How'd you come to know all that play, Uncle Kel?"

"Hit used to be done on Old Christmas when I was a kid. The old folks showed us how."

"Kel and me," said Granny, "we're the only ones left that know it. We say it over to one another regular, whenever Christmas time sets in, just to keep it from pintblank fadin' out of mind. — That first song the boys sang: now that don't really belong in the mummin' play. Hit was Steve's idea to sing it."

Tom and two clean-faced mummers joined us again. The boys had settled themselves on the floor near the hearth and up against the chimney corners. Steve and another big boy brought in a huge green-oak log for the fire.

"You young 'uns better go on back home now," spoke up Sarah. "The show's over."

"We want to hear Rob tell 'Gallymanders,'" said Rhody. "Sue and Helen been askin' me for it, and I told 'em Rob would tell it for us."

"Tell 'Wicked John and the Devil'!" This from Steve.

"No, I'll tell 'Gallymanders' first before them least young 'uns go to sleep and have to be toted home."

As Old Robin drifted into the tale his voice threw out a widening circle of magic until even the littlest young 'uns hushed, were absorbed, gone far away into another world. The older people watched the children's faces in quiet and tender amusement.

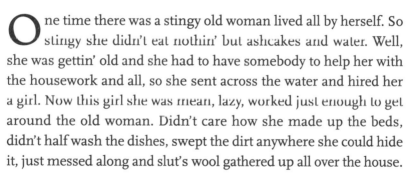

GALLYMANDERS!
GALLYMANDERS!

One time there was a stingy old woman lived all by herself. So stingy she didn't eat nothin' but ashcakes and water. Well, she was gettin' old and she had to have somebody to help her with the housework and all, so she sent across the water and hired her a girl. Now this girl she was mean, lazy, worked just enough to get around the old woman. Didn't care how she made up the beds, didn't half wash the dishes, swept the dirt anywhere she could hide it, just messed along and slut's wool gathered up all over the house.

Now, the old woman had to go to the store one day. Hit was a right far piece from where she lived at. So she told that girl she was goin', told her what work she wanted done up 'fore she got back. Then she says to her, says, "And while I'm gone don't ye dare look up the chimney." Then she threw her bonnet on her head and put out.

So that girl she peeked out the door and watched till the old woman was good and gone, then she ran right straight to the fireplace, hunkered down on the hearthrock, and looked up the chimney. Saw a big long leather bag up there on the smokeshelf. Took the poke-stick and gouged it down. Grabbed it up and jerked it open. It was full of big silver dollars and twenty-dollar gold pieces. Well, that girl she took it and broke and run. Out the door she flew. Ran down the road a piece, then she took out across the pasturefield. Came to an old horse standin' out there.

"Good girl! Good girl! Please rub my old sore back. Rub it for me and I'll ride ye."

"I ain't goin' to dirty my pretty white hands. I'm rich! Got no time to fool with ye." And on she went. Came to an old cow.

"Good girl! Good girl! Please milk my old sore bag. Milk me and strip me, and you can have some milk."

"Ain't goin' to dirty my pretty hands. Got no time to fool with such as you. I'm rich now." She went right on. Came to a peach tree.

"Good girl! Good girl! Please pull off these sprouts so they won't choke me so bad. Just prune me a little and you can eat some of my peaches."

"Ain't goin' to do it! But I'm goin' to eat me some peaches anyhow." And she cloomb up in the peach tree, commenced eatin' off all the good ripe peaches. Eat so many she got sleepy and went on off to sleep sittin' up there in the forks of that tree.

Well, the old woman she got back late that evenin', went in the house and hollered for that girl; and when nobody answered she jumped over there and looked up the chimney, and saw her moneybag was gone. She throwed up her hands and run 'round jest a-squawlin'. Took out the door and run around the house till she saw which-a-way that girl's tracks went, and down the road she put—a-hollerin' every breath:

> *"Gallymanders! Gallymanders!*
> *All my gold and silver's gone!*
> *My great long moneypurse!"*

Came to the horse —

> *"Seen a little gal go by here,*
> *with a jig and a jag*
> *and a long leather bag*
> *and all my gold and silver?"*

"Yes, ma'm!" says the old horse. "Come on! I'll show ye which-a-way she went." So the horse and the old woman went gallopin' off across that pasturefield, the old woman's skirts jest a-floppin'. Came to the fence and the old woman scooted under it and on she went.

> *"Gallymanders! Gallymanders!*
> *All my gold and silver's gone!*
> *My great long moneypurse!"*

Came to the cow —

"Seen a little gal go by here,
with a jig and a jag
and a long leather bag
and all my gold and silver?"

"Yes, ma'm!" says the cow. "She went right yonder way. You'll soon catch her." On she run.

"Gallymanders! Gallymanders!
All my gold and silver's gone!
My great long moneypurse!"

Came to the peach tree —

"Seen a little gal go by here,
with a jig and a jag
and a long leather bag
and all my gold and silver?"

"Yes, *ma'm!*" says the peach tree. "She's up here right now. You want her?"

"Yes, I want her," says the old woman.

So the peach tree bent over and dropped that girl out — bumped her right flat on the ground. And the old woman grabbed her and snatched back that moneypurse, and then she took hold on the girl and shook her around considerable, pulled a switch and switched her legs till she run her off from there. Went on home and hid her moneybag back up the chimney.

Well, the old woman she stayed by herself a right long time but she couldn't get her work done up, so she fin'lly sent over the ocean again and hired her another girl. Now this girl was all right: good hand to work. Holp the old woman right well. She never let a shred of slut's wool gather up anywhere in the house. But the old woman treated her awful mean. Wouldn't let her have a thing to eat hardly, kept pilin' more 'n more work on her; but the girl she done the best she could, never said nothin', just worked right on.

So it wasn't long till the old lady she had to go out to the store again. Called that girl, told her what'n-all to do 'fore she got back, says, "And while I'm gone don't ye dare look up the chimney. Ye hear?" And off she went.

Well, that girl she went on about her work: milked the cow and fed the pig and the chickens, washed the dishes and scoured the pots, swept all the floors and made up the beds, scrubbed the kitchen floor, dusted, straightened up everything, swept the yard, churned, hoed the garden, split firewood and carried it in — and then she was done. So she got out her knittin' and sat down in front of the fireplace. She tried awful hard not to think about looking up the chimney but she just couldn't keep it off her mind. She stopped her knittin' after a while, bent over — then she pushed back in her chair and commenced knittin' and rockin' again —

"Ain't a-goin' do it! I ain't goin' do it!"

Then she got tired of knittin', let her knittin' rest in her lap and stopped rockin'. "Now what in this world do you reckon she's got hid up that chimney? — No, I ain't goin' to look. Ain't goin' do it! Ain't goin' do it!" Took up her knittin' and rocked some more.

Well, directly she couldn't stand it no longer. "No harm in just lookin'," she says. So she stooped down and looked right square up the chimney.

"Well, what in the world is that old thing?" she says. Took the poke-stick and gouged it down. Opened it up and then she dumped all that gold and silver out in the floor.

"My! Ain't that pretty!" she says. And she got down on the floor and played with all them silver dollars and twenty-dollar gold pieces a while — piled 'em up, made little pens and fences, till fin'lly she got tired of playin'. So she put all the money back in the money-bag and tried to put it back up the chimney, but it wouldn't go. She tried and she tried, but ever' time it 'uld fall back down. Got the shovel in one hand and the poker in the other — push it up again, and down it come. So she gave up and just left it layin' there in the ashes. Then she got to studyin' about the old woman findin' it out on her, and she got so scared she left there a-runnin'.

Got down the road a piece, decided she'd take out across the fields so's not to take any chances on meetin' up with that old woman. Came to the horse.

"Good girl! Good girl! Please rub my old sore back. They rode me so hard yesterday, made my old back awful sore. You rub it for me, and I'll ride ye."

"Well, I'm in a hurry, but I reckon I can do that."

So she pulled her a big handful of grass and rubbed the old horse good. Then he took her up on his back and rode her plumb to the end of the field. She jumped off and on she went. Came to the cow.

"Good girl! Good girl! Please milk my old sore bag. They never milked me this mornin' and my old bag's a-hurtin' me so bad. Milk me and you can have some to drink."

"Well, I'm sort of in a hurry, but I reckon I can do that much for ye."

So she milked the old cow in a little shiny tin bucket was there by the fence. Stripped her good and dry. Had her a drink of milk, and on she went. Came to the peach tree.

"Good girl! Good girl! Please pull off these sprouts. They're chokin' me so bad. You prune me a little and you can have some of my peaches."

"Well, now, I really oughtn't to stop but I reckon I can do it for ye."

So she broke off all the sprouts. Then the peach tree says to her, says, "Now, you climb on up here and get all the ripe peaches you want; and if that old woman comes by here, don't you worry none. I'll handle her."

That girl she hadn't had nothin' to eat but ashcakes and water for I don't know how long and them peaches looked awful good. So she cloomb on up to where she could sit easy-like in the forks of the tree, pulled her off a ripe peach and commenced eatin'.

Well, the old woman got back, run in the house and hollered for that girl, and when the girl never answered, the old woman run quick and looked up the chimney. Throwed back her hands and commenced slappin' her skirts and hollerin' and runnin' all around inside the house and out, a-lookin' for that girl's tracks. Saw which way she left and put out from there a-squallin':

> *"Gallymanders! Gallymanders!*
> *All my gold and silver's gone!*
> *My great long moneypurse!"*

Traced the girl to where the old horse was at—

> *"Seen a little gal go by here,*
> *with a jig and a jag*
> *and a long leather bag*
> *and all my gold and silver?"*

"Ma'm?" says the old horse, and the old woman she had to say it all over again.

"No'm," says the horse. "Hain't seen a soul for quite a spell."

So on she run—flippity-flop!—and she was commencin' to get out of breath—

> *"Gallymanders! Gallymanders!*
> *All my gold and silver's gone! (a-heh!)*
> *My great long moneypurse!"*
> *Came to the cow—*

> *"Seen a little gal go by here,*
> *with a jig and a jag (heh!)*
> *and a long leather bag (heh!)*
> *and all my gold and silver?"*

"Well, now, ma'm," says the cow, "I been right here all evenin' and I ain't seen hardly nobody go by here at all, ma'm."

So the old woman run right on—and she was a-givin' out every step—

> *"Gallymanders! Gallymanders! (heh!)*
> *All my gold and silver's gone (a-heh!)*
> *My great long moneypurse! (a-heh-a-heh-a-heh!)"*

Came to the peach tree—

"Seen a little gal (heh!)
go by here (heh!)
with a jig and a jag
and a long leather bag (a-heh-i-heh!)
and all my gold and silver? (a-heh-i-heh-i-heh!)"

"No, ma'm," says the peach tree. "She didn't go by here."

So the old woman went right on a-loopety-loop! — with her skirts a-draggin' and her tongue hangin' out and her a-pantin' ever' breath like an old hound dog—

"Gallymanders! Gallymanders!
(A -heh-i-heh-i-heh!)
All my gold and silver's gone!
(A-heh-i-heh-i-heh!)
My great long moneypurse!
(A — heh — i — heh — i — heh — i — heh!)"

Ran till she give plumb out. Man came along and found her 'side the road where she'd give out at, put her in his dump-truck where he'd been haulin' gravel and took her on back to her house, dumped her out by the gate.

They say she never did try to hire no more girls after that. But I never did hear it told whether she fin'lly looked in the ashes and found her old moneypurse or not. Anyhow, last time I was down there she was still so stingy she wouldn't eat nothin' but ashcakes and water.

Rhody and another big girl gathered up protesting little ones and began sorting out coats and sweaters from the oak chest. As they filed out Rhody turned at the door, "I'm comin' right back. Don't nobody tell 'Whitebear Whittington' till I get here."

"'Wicked John'! 'Wicked John'!" insisted several boys.

"That ain't no tale for young folks," said Sarah.

"Now, Sary, there's folks like Wicked John in this world, and you know it." This was from Granny.

Three boys came from their distant places on the bed and established themselves squarely in front of Old Rob, with their backs to the fire. Two other little girls had claimed the old man's lap as soon as the first two had left with Rhody.

"Kel here ought to be tellin' this 'un. He can tell it better'n me; he learned it to me."

"I ain't got it straight in my mind now," said Uncle Kel, "especially since you put in all that new stuff about Saint Peter. You tell it."

"I learned that Saint Peter part from Tom here. — Well, anyhow — "

WICKED JOHN
AND THE DEVIL

One time there was an old blacksmith that folks called Wicked John. They say he was right mean: never would join the church, never did go to meetin', always laughed about folks gettin' saved and bein' baptized and sech. One thing about him, though, mean as he was, he always did treat a stranger right. And one mornin' a old beggar came along: crippled up, walkin' on two sticks, all bent over with rheumatism, looked right tired and hungry-like. Stood there in the door, and Wicked John fin'lly hollered at him, says, "Come on in! Whyn't ye come on in and sit down?" So the old beggar he heaved over the doorsill, sat down on it, and they talked a while. Wicked John he kept right on workin', talkin' big, and directly he throwed his hammer down and went to the house. Come back with a big plate of vittles: boiled sweet potato, big chunk of ham-meat, greens, beans, big slice of cake, and a glass of sweet milk. Says, "Here, old man! You might make out with these rations — if there's anything here you can eat."

The old beggar thanked him and started in eatin', and old John he went on with his work. Well, he was a-hammerin' around over there, sort of watchin' the beggar man, and pretty soon he saw him lay that plate and the glass to one side and start to get up. He let them two sticks fall to the ground and commenced straightenin' up, straightenin' up, and all the kinks come out of him, till the next thing Wicked John knowed, a big stout-lookin' man was r'ared up there in the door: had a long white beard and white hair, white robe right down to his feet, and a big key in his hand. Old John had done dropped his hammer and was a-standin' there with his mouth hangin' open and his eyes popped out. So the old man says to him, says, "Well, John, I'm Saint Peter. Yes, that's who I am, and once every year I walk the earth to see can I find any decent folks left down here, and the first man treats me right I always give him three wishes. So you can just go ahead now and take your three wishes. Anything you've a mind to, you can just wish for it and hit'll be that-a-way."

Wicked John looked over there at Saint Peter sort of grinnin' like he didn't think it was really so, says, "Well, Peter, you better let me study on it a minute. Three wishes. Aaa Lord!"

Looked around, started wishin' on the first thing popped into his head. He didn't care!

"Well now, I've got a fine old high-back rockin' chair there by the door, and when I get my work done up I like to sit in my rocker; but, don't you know, every day nearly, blame if there ain't somebody done gone and got there ahead of me — one of these loafers hangs around in here of a evenin'.

Makes me mad! And I just wish: — that anybody sits in my old rocker would have to stay there and rock right on till I let 'em get up.

"Aaa Lord! — Lemme see now. — Well, there's my old sledge hammer. It's these blame boys come in here and get to messin' with it, take it out there across the road, see how big a rock they can bust; and — con-found! — if I don't have to go out there ever' time I need it and hunt for it where them feisty boys have done gone and dropped it down in the grass somewhere. And I jest wish: — that anybody teches my sledge hammer would have to pound with it, and keep right on a-poundin' till I let 'em stop."

Well, Saint Peter he looked kind of sorry like he thought old John was a-wastin' his wishes pretty bad, but that old blacksmith he was mean, like I said, just didn't care about nothin' or nobody. Looked around at Saint Peter right mischievous-like, grinned sort of devilish, says, "One more wish, huh? Well, all right. Now: — I got a fine thornbush jest outside the door there, fire bush, gets full of red blooms real early in the spring of the year; and I like my old fire thorn, but — con-found! — ever'body comes here to get their horses shoed, blame if they don't tromple all over that bush, back their wagons into it, break it down; and — Aaa Lord! — these high-falutin' folks comes over the mountain a-fox-huntin' — Humph! fox-huntin' in red coats! — looks like they jest got to have ridin' switches off my bush, break off ridin' switches ever' time they pass. And I jest wish: — anybody *teches* my fire thorn, it 'uld catch 'em and hold 'em right down in the middle of all them stickers till I let 'em out."

Well, Saint Peter he stepped over the doorsill and he was gone from there and Wicked John couldn't tell which-a-way he went nor nothin'.

So that old blacksmith he kept on blacksmithin' in his black-smith shop, and it wasn't long till John and his old woman they got to fussin'. Well, she was jawin' at him and jawin' at him, and he jawed right back at her, till fin'lly she told him, says, "The Devil take ye anyhow, old man! I jest *wish he would!*"

So that day the old man was a-workin' in his shop, looked up and there was a little devil a-standin' in the door, says, "Daddy said he'd take ye now. Said for me to bring ye right on back."

"All right, son. I'll be ready to go with ye in jest a few more licks.

Reckon you can let me finish this horseshoe. Come on in. I'll not be but a minute or two."

Well, the little devil he stepped over in the shop, hung around awhile, and then he went straight and sat down in that old high-back rockin' chair, commenced rockin'. Wicked John he finished the horseshoe, soused it in the coolin' tub, threw it on the ground and picked him up another'n.

"Hey, old man! You said jest finish that one!" And he tried to get out of that rocker, but the more he tried to get up the worse that old chair rocked him, till that little devil's head was just a-goin' *whammity-bang!* against the chairback. And fin'lly he got to beggin' and hollerin' for Wicked John to let him go.

"All right. I'll let ye go if you get on out of here and not bother me no more."

So the little devil said yes, he'd go, and when the chair quit rockin', he jumped out of it and — *a-whippity-cut!* out the door he flew.

Well, not long after that the old woman she lit into the old man again about somethin' or other; and they was a-havin' it! She was just a-fussin', and he was just a-laughin' at her, till fin'lly she stomped around, says, "I'll jest tell ye, old man! The Devil can have ye right now for all I care! He shore can! He can send for ye and take ye off from here, and the sooner the better. That's all there are to it now!" Stomped on out to the kitchen, slammed the door.

So that day another little devil come to the door of the shop, little bigger'n the first 'un, says, "Come on, old man. Daddy sent me for ye. Said for me not to wait for nothin', bring ye right on back. So come on now, and we'll go."

"All right, son. Yes, in-deed. I'm jest about ready. Come in, and I know you'll let me hit a few more licks on this wagon-tire. I'm bound to finish hit 'fore we start."

Well, that little devil he come on inside the shop, got to hangin' around lookin' at what old John was doin', seen he was havin' it kind of awkward the way he had to hold on to that wagon tire and beat it with one hand, says, "Here, old man, you hold it and let me beat it. We got to hurry or Daddy'll get after me for stayin' so long." — Picked up that old sledge hammer layin' there on the ground, started in poundin'.

So Wicked John he held the wagon tire up and turned it where he wanted it fixed, and when it was done he pulled it out from under the hammer between licks, set it against the wall. And when the little devil tried to let go the hammer handle, he just stuck to it and hit a-poundin' right on. Well, the way the old sledge swung that little devil around in there, a-jerkin' him up and down with his legs a-flyin' ever' which-a-way — hit was a sight in this world! So he got to beggin', "Please let me go! Please, sir! Make this thing turn loose of me!"

"All right. I'll let ye go if you get on out of here and don't never come back. Ye hear?"

The little devil said yes, he heard and no, he'd not be back never no more; and then he fell off the hammer-handle and out the door he streaked.

Well, a few days after that the old woman she started raisin' another racket. They hadn't spoke many words 'fore she r'ared back and stuck her hands on her hips, hollered at him, says, "Old man! I jest wish — the *puore — old — Devil* himself would come on and git ye! I shore do! Now you get on out of here 'fore I knock ye in the head with this stick of firewood!"

So old John he dodged the stick of wood and laughed at the old lady, and went on out to his shop, and — sure enough — he hadn't any more'n got started workin' 'fore he looked up and there standin' in the door was the Old Boy himself, with his horns and his tail and that old cow's foot of his'n propped up on the sill, says, "COME ON NOW, OLD MAN! AND I AIN'T A-GOIN' TO TAKE NO FOOL-ISHNESS OFF YE NEITHER!"

"Yes, sir! No, sir! I'm ready to go, mister, right now. I jest got to finish sharpenin' this mattick. Promised a man I'd get it done first thing this mornin'. Come on in and sit down."

"NO! I'LL NOT SIT IN NO CHAIR OF YOUR'N!"

"All right, sir. All right. We'll be ready to go quicker'n you can turn around if you'd jest give this mattick blade a lick or two while I hold it here. There's the sledge hammer leanin' there on the doorsill."

"NO! I AIN'T GOIN' TO TECH NO SLEDGE HAMMER!" says the old Devil. Says, "YOU DONE MADE ME MAD ENOUGH ALREADY, OLD MAN! I DIDN'T LIKE A BIT THE WAY YOU DONE MY BOYS, AND I'M A-TAKIN' YOU OFF FROM HERE RIGHT NOW. YOU HEARD ME!"

And the old Devil reached in and grabbed Wicked John by the back of his collar, started draggin' him out. So old John he started in fightin': punchin', knockin', beatin', poundin', scratchin', kickin', bitin'. They had several rounds there just outside the door, made

the old Devil awful mad, says, "CONFOUND YE, OLD MAN! I'M GOIN' TO LICK THE HIDE OFF YOU RIGHT NOW. JEST SEE IF I DON'T—WHERE'LL I GET ME A SWITCH?"

The old Devil looked around and reached for that bush, and time he touched it, hit grabbed him and wropped around him, jerked him headforemost right down in the middle of that bush where them thorns was the thickest. The old Devil he tried to get loose but the more he thrashed around in there, the worse he got scratched up till fin'lly he just stayed right still, with his legs a-stickin' out the top of the bush.

"Mister?"

"What ye want?"

"Please, sir, let me out of here."

"All right. I'll let ye go on one condition: — you, and none of your boys, don't none of ye never come up here a-botherin' me no more. Ye hear? You promise me that and I might let ye go."

"Heck yes, I'll promise," says the old Devil. "I'll not come, and I'll not send nobody neither—not never no more."

So the bush turned him loose, and sech a kickin' up dust you never did see. The Old Boy left there and he wasn't moseyin' neither.

Well, Wicked John he kept on blacksmithin' and he wasn't bothered by no more devils. And after a long time he died and went on up to the pearly gates. When he got there he knocked, and Saint Peter opened up a little crack, looked out, says, "Oh, it's you, is it? What ye want?"

"Well," old John told him, "I thought I might stand *some* little show of gettin' in up here."

"You? Why, old man, don't you know we got your record in yonder? I'll tell ye right now: I was lookin' at your accounts just the other day; and on the credit side—yes—you have a few entries 'way up at the top of the page; but over on the other side— why, man! hit's filled up right down to the bottom line. There hain't a chance in the world of your gettin' in this place." And Saint Peter started shuttin' the gates to.

So old John turned around and down the stairsteps he went. Got down there on the road to hell, a-staggerin' along with his hands in his pockets a-whistlin'. And when he come in sight of the gates of hell, one of them little devils happened to peek out.

"Daddy! O Daddy! Look a-yonder!"

The old Devil come runnin' and when he saw who it was a-comin', he hollered out, says, "Bar the door, boys! Bar the door!"

Them little devils grabbed the big gates and slammed 'em to quick, turned the key in the lock. So when Wicked John come on up and looked through the bars there stood the old Devil with his young 'uns crowdin' around behind him just a-tremblin'.

"Un-unh!" the old Devil says. "Get on away from here now! No, indeed, you ain't comin' in! I'll not *have* ye! Don't ye come no closter! You just turn around right there now, and put off from here."

Wicked John studied a minute, says, "Well, con-found! I don't know what'n the nation to do now. Saint Peter wouldn't let me in up yonder, and here you've done locked me out. Why, I don't know where to go to!"

So the Devil he looked around, grabbed him up a set of tongs, reached in the furnace, and got holt on a hot coal. Handed it out the bars, says, "Here, old man, you jest take this chunk of fire, and go on off somewhere else, and start you a hell of your own."

Old John he took it; and they tell me that if you go down in the Great Dismal Swamps, you can look out of a night and see a little bob of a light a-movin' along out there. And some folks call it the Jacky-my-lantern, and some call it the will-o'-the-whisp — but I reckon you know now who it is.

There was a lively burst of laughter from all the boys; and one of the three in front of Old Robin flung himself head-over-heels in his laughing fit much to the delight of us all.

"Hit's wrong, tellin' these boys such a pack of foolishness," said Sarah. "Them old tales ought to be left alone anyhow."

"Humpf!" went Granny London. "You listened as hard as the kids did the other day when I told 'em what I remembered about Poll and Betts and Mutsmag."

"Tell it! Tell it!" came from the children.

"Deely here knows it better'n me now. I'm forgetful and liable to leave out part of it. You tell it for 'em, Deely."

Delia looked around, and then let her chin sink thoughtfully. "Well, the way I've always heard it told — "

MUTSMAG

One time there was an old woman had three girls, Poll and Betts and Mutsmag. Mutsmag she was the youngest, and Poll and Betts they treated her awful mean, made her do all the work while they'd lie in the bed of a mornin', didn't give her nothin' to eat but left-overs.

Well, the old woman died and all she had was a cabbage patch and an old case-knife. She left the patch of cabbage to Poll and Betts, and she didn't leave Mutsmag nothin' but that old knife. Poll and Betts started in eatin' that cabbage, didn't let Mutsmag have a bite of it. And directly they eat it all up. So then Poll and Betts they decided they'd go a great journey and seek their fortune, so they borryed some meal to make journey cakes. Mutsmag begged and begged couldn't she please go too, and they told her no, she couldn't, but she begged and begged till fin'lly they told her, said, "All right, you crazy thing, but you'll have to fix your own journey cakes. Here, go get you some water in this."

And they handed her a riddel.[1] So Mutsmag took the riddel and ran down to the spring. Tried to dip her up some water, it 'uld run out. Dip it up, it 'uld all run out. Then a little bluebird lit on a limb, tilted over and watched her; and directly it started in singin', says:

> *"Stop it with moss and stick it with clay,*
> *then you can pack your water away!*
> *Stop it with moss and stick it with clay,*
> *then you can pack your water away!"*

"Much obliged," says Mutsmag. "I'll try that." So she smeared clay inside the riddel and pulled some moss and daubed hit over the clay and stopped ever' hole. Packed her riddel back to the house plumb full of water. So then her sisters *had* to let her go.

They got down the road a piece, and Poll and Betts started in whisperin' — turned around all at onct, grabbed Mutsmag and tied her to a laurel grub. Snatched her journey cakes and off they run. Mutsmag pulled at the rope and pulled at it; and fin'lly she thought of her old knife and give the rope a rip and aloose it come. So she took out after Poll and Betts.

They looked back directly and there come Mutsmag. "Law! There's that crazy thing again! What'll we do with her this time?" Well, there was an old shop-house right there 'side the road. So they grabbed her and shoved her in that old shop-house.[2] The door-latch was on the outside, so when Poll and Betts slammed the door on Mutsmag there wasn't no way for her to get out. She tried and tried but she couldn't. So finally she set in to hollerin'. Old fox heard her and come to the door.

---

1. A riddel — an old-time sifter-thing all full of holes, where you strain something through it.

2. Shop-house — that's an old-time place where you fixed wagons and plows and guns. Had a forge and an anvil in it.

"Who's in there?"

"Hit's me — Mutsmag."

"What ye want?"

"I want out."

"Unlatch the latch."

"Ain't none. Hit's out there. See can't you push it up."

"What'll ye give me?"

"I'll take ye to the fat of a goose's neck."

So the fox he reached for the latch and pushed it up, and Mutsmag took him where the fat goose was at, and then she put out and caught up with Poll and Betts again.

"Law! Yonder comes that crazy thing! What in the world will we do with her now?"

"Let's make out she's our servin' girl and make her do all the work when we stay the night somewhere."

So they let Mutsmag alone. And about dark they come to a house and hollered and an old woman come out. They asked her could they stay the night. Says, "We got us a servin' girl. She'll do up all the work for ye."

The old woman said yes, they could stay, so Poll and Betts went on in and sat by the fire and Mutsmag went to scourin' the pots.

Now the old woman had three girls about the size of Poll and Betts and Mutsmag, and she sent 'em all up in the loft to sleep. So they cloomb up the ladder and laid down in the straw, went right to sleep — all but Mutsmag. She stayed awake and listened. Heard somebody come in directly, stompin' around and fussin' at the old woman about supper not bein' ready. Mutsmag looked down quick through the cracks and knotholes, seen it was a giant.

"Hush! Hush!" the old woman told him. "You'll wake up them three fine fat pullets I got for ye up in the loft." Says, "You can get 'em down now and I'll cook 'em for ye."

"HOW'LL I KNOW 'EM FROM YOUR GIRLS?"

"My girls got nightcaps on."

Mutsmag reached right quick and jerked the nightcaps off them three girls, put 'em on her and Poll and Betts, laid back down and went to snorin'. The old giant reached up through the scuttlehole and felt around for the girls that didn't have no nightcaps on. Pulled 'em down out the loft, wrung their necks and throwed 'em over to the old woman. She went to put 'em in the cook-pot, and when she seen what the old giant had done she lit into him with the pot-ladle and nearly beat him to death.

"You ugly old coot!" she hollered at him. "You've gone and got the wrong ones!" And she hit him over the head again. Well, she went to battlin' the old giant with that ladle and the shovel and the poker and whatever she could grab up to beat him with and he went to dodgin' around; and while all that was goin' on, Mutsmag took her old knife and ripped the bedclothes and tied knots and made her a rope. Then she knocked a big hole in the shingles, tied the rope to a rafter and throwed it out, and Poll and Betts and her got away.

Well, they traveled on and traveled on, and the next evenin' they come to the King's house, and he invited 'em in to stay the night. Poll and Betts went to braggin' about what'n-all they done at the old giant's place, made like they was the ones done it. Mutsmag never said a word.

And directly the King said to Poll and Betts, says, "All right. You girls ought to be sharp enough to go back over there and get shet of both of 'em. That old woman's a witch and she's worse than her old man, even if he is a giant. Reckon you can do that for me?"

Of course Poll and Betts couldn't back out then, so they said sure, they could do that. Left there the next mornin', but instead of goin' anywhere close to that giant's place they took out in another direction and that was the last anybody ever seen of 'em.

Well, Mutsmag she never said nothin'. Stayed on there and worked for the King. Then one evenin' she put out and went on down to the giant's house. Had a half-bushel poke of salt with her. So she cloomb up on the old giant's house, got up there next to the chimney, and everwhen the old woman raised the pot-lid

Mutsmag sprinkled salt down in the pot of meat she had cookin'. So directly the old giant started in eatin'.

"OLD WOMAN, THE MEAT'S TOO SALTY!"

"Why, I never put in but one pinch!"

"YOU MUST A' PUT IN A HALF-BUSHEL, OLD WOMAN! FETCH ME SOME WATER HERE!"

"There hain't a bit of water up."

"GO TO THE SPRING AND GET SOME! HURRY NOW! I'M JEST ABOUT DEAD FOR WATER!"

"Hit's too dark."

"THROW OUT YOUR LIGHT-BALL!"

So the old woman threwed her light-ball out toward the spring, but Mutsmag was standin' there and caught it on the point of her old knife; and when the old woman came runnin' with the water bucket, Mutsmag squinched the light-ball in the spring and the old woman stumped her toe and fell and broke her neck. So Mutsmag cut off her head with that old knife, took it on back to the King.

He gave her a bushel of gold, says, "I declare, Mutsmag! You're pretty sharp." Says, "That old giant now, he's got a fine white horse he stole from me. Hit's a ten-mile-stepper, and I been tryin' ever' way in the world to get that horse back. You get it for me and I'll pay ye another bushel of gold."

So Mutsmag she went on back about the time it was gettin' dark. Had her apron pocket full of barley. Went in the stable and there was the fine white horse. Hit had bells on its halter, and the rope where it was tied was awful thick and had more knots in it than you could count. Well, Mutsmag, she took her old knife and went to cuttin' on them knots and the horse throwed up his head—

"Dingle! Dingle!"

The old giant come a-runnin' and Mutsmag hid under the trough. The giant he opened the stable door, looked around, went on back.

So Mutsmag threw some barley in the trough. The horse went for it and them bells didn't dingle so loud.

Mutsmag she started in on them knots again. But the horse eat up all that barley, throwed up his head—

"Dingle! Dingle!"

And here come the old giant! Mutsmag hid by the door. The giant he shoved the door back on Mutsmag, came right on in the stable, looked around, looked around, went on back. Mutsmag throwed a double-handful of barley in the trough and worked at them knots just as hard as she could tear, but the fine white horse got the barley eat up, throwed his head around—

"Dingle! Dingle!"

And the old giant come so fast Mustmag just did have time to jump and hide under the bresh of the fine white horse's tail. Giant came on in, had a lantern with him, looked around, looked under the trough, jerked the door back and looked there, looked in all the corners, up in the rafters. Then he got to feelin' around under the horse's belly, stooped down, shined his lantern, looked, says, "HOLD ON NOW, MY FINE WHITE HORSE! YE GOT TOO MANY LEGS BACK HERE!"

And just about that time the fine white horse switched his tail and there was Mutsmag. She made for the door but the old giant grabbed her, says, "NOW I GOT YE!"

"What you goin' to do with me?"

"DON'T KNOW YET. HAIN'T MADE UP MY MIND!"

"Please don't feed me on honey and butter, I just can't stand the taste of honey and butter."

"THAT'S THE VERY THING I'M GOIN' TO DO! HONEY AND BUTTER IS ALL YOU'LL GIT!"

So he locked her up in the chicken house, gave her all the honey and butter she could hold. Mutsmag jest loved honey and butter. She got fat in a hurry. He come to get her fin'lly, reached in and grabbed her by the leg, toted her on to the house, says, "NOW I'M GOIN' TO KEEL YE!"

"How you goin' to kill me?" Mutsmag asked him.

"DON'T KNOW. HAIN'T MADE UP MY MIND!"

"Please don't put me in a sack and beat me to death, 'cause I'd howl like a dog, and I'd squall like cats, and my bones 'uld crack and pop like dishes breakin', and my blood 'uld run and drip like honey."

"THAT'S THE VERY WAY I'M GOIN' TO KEEL YE!"

So he got a big sack and tied Mutsmag in it. Went on out to cut him a club. Time he got good and gone Mutsmag took her old knife and give that sack a rip and a-loose it come. Then she sewed it back right quick and put the giant's old dog in there and as many cats as she could catch and all the old giant's dishes, and she went and got the biggest pot of honey he had and put hit in, too. Then she went and hid.

The old giant come in directly with a big club — looked like he'd pulled him up a good-sized white oak. Drawed back and lammed into that sack. The dog howled and them cats set in to squallin'. The old giant went to grinnin'.

"O YES! I'LL MAKE YE HOWL LIKE DOGS AND SQUALL LIKE CATS!"

Hit it a few more licks and all them cups and saucers and plates and bowls and pitchers started crackin' and poppin'.

"O YES! I'LL MAKE YOUR BONES POP AND CRACK LIKE DISHES!"

Beat right on, and directly the honey started dribblin' out.

"O YES! I'LL MAKE YOUR BLOOD RUN AND DRIP LIKE HONEY!"

So he hit the sack several more licks and then he untied it and

went to dump Mutsmag out, and there on the floor was his dog killed, and his cats; and ever' dish he had in the house all broke up, and honey jest runnin' all over everything. He was so mad he nearly busted wide open. Throwed down his club and broke and run. Headed right straight for the stable.

But while he was a flailin' that sack, Mutsmag she'd fin'lly got the rope cut, and had left there a-straddle of that fine white horse and him a-hittin' ten miles ever' step. So the old giant looked to see which-a-way they had headed, seen a streak of dust a way off, and he put out. Came to a deep wide river directly, looked across and there was Mutsmag sittin' on a millrock with a rope through the hole and one end tied around her neck.

"HOW'D YOU GIT OVER THAR?"

"I picked a hole in a rock and tied it around my neck and skeeted the rock across."

So the old giant hunted him up a great big flat rock, picked a hole in it and put a length of rope through, and tied it to his neck, and when he tried to skip the rock across hit jerked him in, and that was the last anybody ever saw of him.

So Mutsmag went and got back on the horse where she had him hid in the bresh, rode on back to the King and he paid her two more bushels of gold — one for gettin' his horse and one for gettin' shet of that old giant.

About midway of Delia's tale the two big girls had come back, and now Rhody got the jump on everybody with her choice.

"'Whitebear Whittington'! Please, Deely!" "Give me time to catch my breath, honey. Somebody else tell one. Granny, she knows that."

"You mean 'Three Gold Nuts'?" asked Granny.

"That's it! Tell it!" urged Rhody.

"You tell it, Granny."

"Go on, Deely. You know it."

WHITEBEAR
WHITTINGTON

One time there was a man had three daughters. His wife was dead, and the three girls they kept house for him. And one day he was fixin' to go to town, so he called his girls, asked 'em what did they want him to bring 'em. The oldest told him, says, "I want a silk dress the color of every bird in the sky."

The second girl said, "I want you to bring me a silk dress made out of every color in a rainbow."

The youngest 'un she didn't say anything. So directly he went and asked her didn't she want him to bring her something too. She studied a minute, says, "All I want is some white roses. If you see a white rosebush anywhere you might break me a basketful."

Well, he took him a basket of eggs and got on his horse and went on to town. Got all his tradin' done and started back. Rode on, rode on, come to where there was a thick wilderness of a place, saw a big rosebush 'side the road, full of white roses. So he got off his horse and broke off a few. Thought he heard something behind him, says:

*"You break them
and I'll break you!"*

So he stopped, looked around, waited awhile and tried to see what it was spoke, didn't see anybody nor hear it again, so he broke off some more. Then he heard it real plain—sounded like it was back in the wilderness—

*"You break them
and I'll break you!"*

He started to quit that time, but he still couldn't see anybody or anything, and the prettiest roses were still on the bush, so he reached out his hand to break them off—and that thing said:

*"Give me what meets you
first at the gate,
you can break all you want
till your basket is full."*

He thought a minute or two—and he knew that his old dog always came lopin' out in the road whenever he got in home. The old hound wasn't much good anyway—so he answered, says:

*"Whatever meets me
first at the gate,
you can come take it
whenever you want."*

Went ahead and broke white rosebuds till his basket was full. Got on his horse and rode on in home.

He kept lookin' for his dog to come out but the old hound was up under the house asleep and before he could whistle for it here came his youngest girl flyin' out the gate to meet him.

He hollered to her and motioned her to go back but she wasn't payin' him any mind, came right on. She took his basket and was a-carryin' on over how pretty the roses were. So she thanked him and went to helpin' him unload his saddlebags, and when they got to the house she saw he was lookin' troubled, says, "What's the matter, Daddy?" But he wouldn't tell her.

And he never came to the table when they called him to supper, just sat there on the porch lookin' back down the holler. So the girls they ate their supper, and it got dark directly and they lit the lamp. Sat there sewin' and talkin', and all at once they heard a voice out in the road —

"Send out my pay!"

Their daddy came in the house then, and told 'em what'n-all he had heard when he broke the roses. The oldest girl she said to him, says, "Aw, just send out the dog. How could it know what met you first?"

So they called the dog and sicked him out toward the gate. He ran out barkin' and then they heard him come back a-howlin', scared to death, and he crawled way back under the floor and stayed there. Then they heard it again —

"Send out my pay!"

So the two oldest girls said they wasn't afraid, said they'd go see what it was. Out they went, and directly there was a commotion at the gate and the two girls came tearin' back to the house so scared they couldn't speak. Then it hollered louder —

"Send out my pay!"

Then the youngest girl said, "I'll have to go, Daddy, but don't you worry; I'll come back some way or other."

So she gathered her up a few things in a budget and kissed her father and went on out to the gate. There stood a big white bear.

"Get up on my back," it told her. So she crawled up on its back and it started off.

The girl was cryin' so hard her nose bled and three drops of blood fell on the white bear's back. They went on, went on, and 'way up in the night she made out how they went past a big white rosebush out in a thick wilderness. Came to a fine house out there and the white bear stopped, told her, "Get off now."

So she got off and went on in the house. The white bear came in behind her, says, "Light that lamp there on the table." So she lit the lamp, and when she turned back around there stood a good-lookin' young man. The minute she looked at him she thought the world of him. He said to her then, says, "This house and everything in it belongs to you now, and there's nothing here to hurt you."

Then he took the lamp and they went through all the rooms lookin' at all the fine things, and directly they came to a pretty bedroom and he told her, says, "Now I got a spell on me and I can't be a man but part of the time. From now on I can be a man of a night and stay with you here and be a bear of a day, or I can be a bear of a night and sleep under your bed and be a man of a day. Which had you rather I'd be?"

So she thought about it and she didn't like the idea of a bear layin' under her bed of a night so she told him she'd rather he'd be a man of a night. So that was the way it was. He was a bear in the daytime and he'd lie around outside while she kept house, and when dark came he'd be a man. He kept plenty of wood and water in the house and they'd talk together and he was good company.

So they kept on and she lived happy even if her husband did have to be a bear half the time. He told her how it was he'd been witched, said he'd get out of it some day but he didn't know just how it would be. And after three or four years she had three little babes, two boys and a girl. Then when her least one was big enough to walk she told her husband she wanted to go back to see her father again. It looked like that troubled him but he told her all right, they would go; but he said she would have to promise him not to tell anybody anything about him, and *never* to speak his name.

"If you speak my name to any living soul I'll have to go away. And you will see me going off up the mountain and it will be awful hard for us ever to get together again."

So she promised him and early the next mornin' he took her and the three children on his back, and he let them off at her father's gate and she took her babes and went on to the house.

They were all proud to see her again and told her how pretty her children were and commenced askin' her who her husband was and where they lived and all. She told 'em she couldn't tell. Well, they kept on at her and she kept tellin' 'em she couldn't possibly tell, so her sisters they started actin' mad and wouldn't speak to her. Still she wouldn't tell; but the next day her daddy took her aside and spoke to her about it, says, "Just tell me his name."

She thought surely she ought to tell her own father what her man's name was, so she whispered it to him —

"Whitebear Whittington."

And she hadn't but spoke it when she looked up and saw her husband and he was in the shape of a man, and he was goin' off up the Piney Mountain, and on the back of his white shirt were three drops of blood.

Well, she loved him; so she left the children there with her father and started out to try and find her man again. She took out the way he went over the Piney Mountain but she never did see him on ahead of her. But she went on and went on. Sometimes she'd think she was lost but a white bird would fly over and drop a white feather with a red speck on it, so she'd go on the way that bird was headed. Then she'd stop at a house to stay the night and

they'd tell her about the fine young man had stayed there the night before, had three drops of blood on his shirt.

So she went on, went on, for seven years and that bird would fly over whenever she got down-hearted, so she didn't give up.

Then late one evening she stopped at a house and called to stay the night and an old, old woman awful stricken in age came to the door, looked like she was over a hundred years old and she was walkin' on two sticks, told her to come on in. The old woman looked at her, says, "Girl, you're in bad trouble, now ain't ye?"

So she told the old lady about what'n-all had happened, and how she'd been tryin' to find her man again; and directly the old woman told her, says, "You just stay here with me now, and get rested up a little, and it may be I can help you. I got a lot of wool to work and I need somebody. Will you stay and help me about my wool?"

She said yes, she would. So the next day they got all the fleeces out and she helped pick out the burs and trash, and washed the wool in the creek, while the old woman carded. Carded so fast the girl had a time keepin' up with her and they got it all done by sundown. And that night the old woman gave her a gold chinquapin. The next day the girl she helped with the spinnin': handed the rolls of carded wool to the old lady, and it was a sight in the world how she could spin. They got it all spun up about dark, and that night the old woman handed her a gold hickory nut. Then the third day the old woman she sat down at her loom and the girl kept fixin' the bobbins and handin' 'em to her and the old loom went *click! wham! click! wham!* all day long, and just 'fore dark the weavin' was all done. So that night the old woman gave her a gold walnut, says, "Now you keep these three gold nuts and don't you crack 'em till you're in the most trouble you could ever be in. And if the first one don't get ye out, crack the next, and if you have to crack the last 'un you surely ought to be out of your trouble by then."

So she thanked the old lady and the next mornin' she left with the three gold nuts in her apron pocket. She went on, went on, and in three days she came to a river and she went along the river till she came to a washin' place where a great crowd of young women was gathered, and there in the middle of all them women she saw her husband. She got through the crowd and went up to him but when he looked at her it was just as if he never had known her before in all his life.

He didn't have any shirt on and she saw the women lined up before the washin' place and one girl was down on her knees washin' his shirt with all her might. She listened and heard 'em talkin' about how that young man had said he'd marry the one could wash the blood out of his shirt. So she got in the line and fin'lly got down to the washin' place. The one ahead of her was a big stout woman and she was down on her knees a-washin' that shirt so hard it looked like she'd tear it apart. Soap it and maul it with the battlin' stick and rinse it and soap it and maul it again, but the blood just got darker and darker. So directly the girl said she'd like to have her turn. That other woman didn't get up off her knees, looked at her, says, "Humph! If I can't get this blood out I know a puny thing like you can't do it."

Well, that girl she just leaned down and took hold on his shirt and gave it one rub and it was white as snow. But before she could turn around the other woman grabbed it and ran with it, says, "Look! Look! I washed it out!"

So the young man he had to go home with her.

His real wife knew now that she was in the most trouble she could ever be in. So she followed 'em and saw what house it was, and about dark she went there, went right in the door and cracked her gold chinquapin. It coiled out the finest gold wool you ever saw —just one long carded roll ready to be spun. So she started pullin' out the gold wool and pretty soon that other woman came in and saw it, says, "Oh, I must have that! What will you take for it?"

"Why, I couldn't part with my gold nut."

"You name any price you want now, and I'll give it to ye."

"Let me stay this night with your man and you can have it."

"Well! I must have that gold chinquapin. You go on out and wait till I call ye."

So she took the gold chinquapin and put it away. Then she put a sleepy pillow on the young man's bed and just before he went to go to bed she gave him a sleepy dram, and then she called that girl, and when she went in to him he was sound asleep. She sat down beside him and tried to wake him up but he slept right on. So she stayed there by him all night cryin' and singin':

> *"Three drops of blood I've shed for thee!*
> *Three little babes I've born for thee!*
> *Whitebear Whittington! Turn to me!"*

And when daylight came that other woman made her leave. Well, the girl came back that next evening and broke the gold hickory nut. A fine spinning wheel came out of it, stood right up in the floor and started spinnin'. All you had to do was put the gold chinquapin in a crack in the logs and set the end of the wool on the spindle, and it spun right on — spin and wind, spin and wind all by itself. Hit was the finest gold thread you ever saw. And when that woman came in and saw it, said she just had to have the wheel. So the girl let her have it for another night with her man. But when she went to him he slept right on through the night because that sleepy pillow was still under his head and that woman had gone and given him another sleepy dram. So all night his wife stayed by him tryin' to wake him up —

> *"Three drops of blood I've shed for thee!*
> *Three little babes I've born for thee!*
> *Whitebear Whittington! Turn to me!"*

And early in the morning that other woman came, said, "Get on out now. Your time is up."

Well, the next evening the father of that woman called the young man just before bedtime. Said he wanted to have a word with him. So they walked out a ways and the old man said to him, says, "I couldn't sleep a bit the last two nights. There's some kind of a cryin' noise been goin' on in your room, and somebody singin' a mournful song right on up through the night."

The young man said he had slept uncommon sound the last two nights, hadn't heard a thing.

"Well now," says the old man, "I want you to be sure to stay awake tonight, and listen and see what all that carryin' on is."

So that night the girl came and cracked the gold walnut and a big loom came out of it — just r'ared up in the house time she broke the nut. It was warped with gold warp and all you had to do was feed it bobbins of that gold thread and it wove right on — all by itself. The woman she heard it a-beatin' and she came running.

"Oh, my! I must have that! What'll you take for your loom?"

The girl told her.

"Well!" she says, real hateful-like, "You can stay with him tonight but I'll tell ye right now it's the last time."

So she made the girl go out and then she looked about that sleepy pillow bein' still on the bed, went and fixed that sleepy dram, made it real strong, and when the young man came in to go to bed she handed it to him, made him drink it; but he kept it in his mouth and when she left he spit it out. Then he looked at that pillow and threw it off the bed. Laid down and closed his eyes. The woman she looked in at him to make sure he was asleep, then she let that girl in. She came in the room and saw him there with his eyes shut and her grief nearly killed her. She didn't know what she'd do. She came and sat on the edge of the bed and put her hand on his shoulder and started cryin':

> "Three drops of blood I've shed for thee!
> Three little babes I've born for thee!
> Whitebear Whittington! — "

Well, time she called his name he opened his eyes and turned to her, and then he knew her. So he put his arms around her, and they went on to sleep.

The next morning that other woman came and found the door

locked and she was mad as time. And after they got up, the young man he came and called that woman's father, said, "Let's step outside. I want a word with *you.*"

So they went out and he told the man, says, "If you had a lock and a key, and the key fitted the lock perfect, and you lost that key and got a new one; then you found the old key again, and it fitted the lock much better than the new one — which key would you keep?"

The old man answered him, says, "Why, I'd keep the old one."

"Well," says the young man, "I found my old wife last night and she suits me a lot better than your daughter does, so you can just have her back."

So they left and got their three children and went on home, and that spell on him was broke so he never was a bear again, and they lived happy.

"Now that's one tale I always did like," admitted Sarah.

Uncle Kel spoke up: "Speakin' about these tales comin' down from old times — did ye ever hear that 'un about the boy that killed the King's deer?"

Jeems, who knew my constant and hopeful search for Robin Hood ballads, shot me a grin as I looked up from my yellow pad, flexed my fingers, and picked up my pencil again.

"There used to be a King over this country," stated Old Kel, "and I reckon this tale must be an old one. Hit must'a happened before the battle of King's Mountain. Well, anyway — "

THE OUTLAW BOY

The king claimed he had a lot of deer out in the wilderness places, and he made a law that anybody who shot his deer would be hung. Now this young feller in the tale—Robin, that was his name—he had been out a right smart with the Indians and had got to be an awful good hand with the bow 'n arrow. He was a good shot: knock a dead center a hundred steps off. He liked to go out in the woods after wild turkeys and squirrels, but he never had bothered none of the King's deer.

Then one day he was out in the mountains and he met up with a deputy sheriff. They walked along together a piece and they got to talkin' about shootin', and directly they tried some shots. The deputy he'd draw his gun and shoot, come right close to the mark, but that boy would pull his arrow back and hit it right square in the center ever' time. That riled the deputy sheriff, havin' a young feller like that outdo him with a bow 'n arrow, but he never let on.

So directly they looked out down a holler and saw a deer feedin'

about a hundred yards from where they were at. The deputy says to him, says, "I'll bet ye twenty dollars you can't hit that deer yonder."

"Oh, no. I'll not shoot no deer."

"Go ahead. I'll not arrest ye. Anyhow, you can't hit it from here."

"I won't break the law, I'll tell ye that right now."

"If you happen to hit it, I'll not turn ye in; not never mention it. Are ye afraid to bet?"

"Put up your money!" Rob told him; and they laid twenty dollars apiece there on a stump.

So Robin drawed his bow and when he let loose the arrow that deer dropped right in its tracks. He reached down to take the money and that deputy grabbed him, says, "Now I got ye! You'll hang for this sure. You got no witness, and they'll take my word against your'n."

They scuffled around and the boy throwed him, and then the deputy reached for his gun, so Robin grabbed his bow and had an arrow on it quicker'n you could turn around and time the deputy sheriff drawed on him Robin shot him in the arm, and that deputy got up and ran off from there as fast as his legs 'uld carry him.

Well, that boy knowed he'd get into trouble if he went back to the settlements, so he decided he'd live in the wilderness. And it wasn't long till several others who'd got in trouble with the King one way or another j'ined Robin out there. They built 'em up a good campin' place, and after a while there was a big gang of 'em. They lived off game: killed a deer once in a while, gathered berries and nuts, and they did fairly well. They couldn't get no powder nor lead, so they all made bows and arrows and they got to be as good shots with them as anybody else with long-rifles. Hit got to be known all over the country about them bein' such dead shots with the bow 'n arrow.

Now that King had caused such hard times in the country that Rob and his gang went to takin' stuff from rich folks that came through on the public road and would give it to them that needed it. So fin'lly they lived pretty good out there, and all the poor people who knew where they camped at wouldn't tell it. The high sheriff of that county he 'uld try to catch some of 'em, but they always went out several in a bunch and folks 'uld warn 'em in time 'fore any posse got anywhere close. Then they'd hide out and shoot at the sheriff and his men and scare 'em right bad; so pretty soon they just quit tryin' to arrest any of that wilderness outfit.

Then one mornin' some of 'em was walkin' along and they looked out one side the road and saw a woman sittin' on a log a-cryin'. Asked her what was the matter, and she told 'em that her two sons had been arrested for killin' a deer and were goin' to be hung that very day at ten o'clock in the courthouse square. She said she was a widow and they were so poor they hadn't nothin' to eat, and her boys had taken a chance on killin' a deer but had got caught 'fore they got in home with the meat.

"Never you mind about that, ma'm," Rob told her. "You can just cheer up now, and go on back home. If anybody gets hung at ten o'clock, hit'll not be your boys, because I'm the one that's goin' to do any hangin' that's done today."

So the old lady she cheered up and left.

Then Robin he fixed it up with his men to hide out near the courthouse with their bows and plenty of arrows, and he told 'em that when he blowed his horn they were to come a-runnin'. Told 'em to go on and get ready. Said he was goin' on ahead by himself.

So Robin went on toward town, got out in the main road and directly there came an old beggar, bowin' to him, bowin', and takin' off his hat. He had on an old jingly suit of clothes, coat all tore to pieces. He was awful honery-fixed.

"Howdy do, daddy."

"Good mornin', sir. Good mornin', sir."

"How'd you like to swap clothes with me?"

"Aw, you don't want my old ragged fixin's."

"I might too now. You pull off and we'll change right here."

So the old beggar and Rob swapped clothes, and he gave the old man some money to boot. That pleased him awful well. Then Robin asked him, says, "Do you know who I am?"

"Why, no, I don't know ye."

"I'm the head of that wilderness gang, and you better stay out of sight today. They might take you for me and shoot ye."

So the old beggar man he headed for the woods, scared to death, and hid out, and Robin went on toward town. He looked out before him directly and here came the high sheriff ridin' on a big fine horse. So Robin commenced bowin' to him, bowin' to him, till he rode up. Then Rob he made like he wanted to speak to him. The sheriff pulled up his horse, says, "What you want?" — Talked awful hateful.

"I need me some clothes — bad. Hain't you got an old suit you can give me?"

"No! I got no time to fool with ye. I got to hire somebody to do a hangin' for me today. I been huntin' since early this mornin' for a man that'll take the job, and it's almost time for the hangin' right now."

"I'll hire to hang."

"You will? All right, then. You can have the clothes off the two men bein' hung, and I'll pay ye two dollars for the job."

"That'll suit me all right, I reckon."

"Well, come on, you old fool. We'll have to hurry."

The sheriff rode on off, and left Robin to walk. And when Rob got to the courthouse the sheriff had them two young fellers up on the scaffle and the nooses already around their necks.

"Come on here, old man, and get this done. Be quick about it!"

Rob looked around, says, "Ain't there no preacher here to pray for these fellers 'fore we hang 'em?"

"No. We got no time for any such foolishness. Come on here and pull the trap."

"Oh, no, sir, not before we have some preachin' done. I know where I can get us a lot of preachers. I can get 'em here right quick for ye."

So Robin pulled out his horn from under that old ragged coat and blowed it, and all his men jumped out with their bows drawn on the sheriff and all his deputies and came at 'em. The crowd that was there to see the hangin' commenced shoutin' and hollerin' and laughin' to see the high sheriff in such a fix, and the sheriff and his men saw the danger they were in and had to back down. Then Robin he took the ropes off the two young men and told 'em to go on back home and let their mother see they were all right.

Then Rob he took hold on the high sheriff and dragged him up on the scaffle, put the noose around his neck, says, "I said I'd do your hangin' today, didn't I?" Says, "I'd sure like to have that suit of clothes you got on, too. — You ready to pull the trap, boys?"

So they kept on foolin' with the ropes and the trap, a-mak-in' out like they would hang the sheriff and he kept beggin' 'em not to do it. Then Robin says to him, says, "I'll make ye a proposition now: you promise you'll not bother them two boys no more and not take up any more men for deer-killin', and we might let ye off, this time."

The sheriff he promised quick. He was just a-sweatin'.

"And you can tell the King, too, if he interferes with these two boys, or us either, I'll call my men and we'll raise an army and hang him and all his deputies. There's a lot of folks don't care much for the way he's been runnin' things."

So the sheriff agreed to that, too, and Robin turned him loose and he and his men they left there in a hurry.

"We're through, boys. Let's go on back to headquarters."

So they all went on back to the wilderness, and the law quit botherin' 'em.

Then that mean King he fin'lly got put out of office, and they had a good King who tried to make better laws and run the nation right, but word was slow gettin' out to that part of the country where Robin and his gang lived, and there were lowdown deputies and severe tax-assessors still runnin' over the people in that section.

So Robin and his men they still saw fit to take from the rich and give to the poor. And one day Rob was out huntin' when he saw a brisk-lookin' man comin' along on a horse. Looked like a real rich man, so Robin got out before him, drawed his bow and stopped him, says, "Hand here your money, ever' cent of it."

That man reached in his saddle-pockets and started handin' over his money.

"Look in your clothes, too. I want to know how much you got on ye."

Well, when the man started reachin' in his pockets, his coat folded back and Robin saw by the badge on him that it was the King. So he took all the money and handed it back to him. — Hit wasn't so much — not more'n a travelin' man 'uld need anyhow.

"No. I'll not take anything off you. I love my King. We've done heard about you out here, and we're glad you've come. I reckon you'll be cleanin' up all the deviltry that's been goin' on in these settle-ments."

"And who are you?" the King asked him.

"My name's Hood — Robin Hood."

"Are you the one that dressed up like a beggar that time, and played such a trick on the sheriff?"

"Yes, I reckon I'm the one."

The old King threw back his head and laughed good, slapped his hand on his knee, says, "Then you're the very man I'm lookin' for. I've heard a lot about you boys — good report, too, accordin' to my way of thinkin'. Heard about you bein' such good shots with the bow 'n arrow and I wanted to see you shoot a little."

"Just come on and we'll go back where my gang is at. We'll fix up a little somethin' to eat first, and then we might do a little shootin' for ye."

So he took the new King right on in to headquarters, says, "Boys, this here man is our new King. Fix up a little dinner for all of us now, and after we eat we'll have a little fun."

They went to it and cooked up all kinds of good deer meat and bear meat and wild turkeys and fish. Baked some big pones of bread, and got dinner all ready. Then they set the King down and they all pulled up their benches, and it was a sight in the world to see them men eat. The King bragged on how good everything was, and they talked politics a little, and they fin'lly got done eatin'. Then they set up some poles and marks a good piece off and went to shootin'. It was hard to say which one was the best.

Then the King says to 'em, says, "I never saw such shootin' in all my life." Says, "Now, boys, I'll tell ye: if you men want to come back under the law again I'll not have ye prosecuted for a thing. Why, I can use ye, ever' man here. I need ye for sheriffs and deputies in this section; and if any of ye want to jine my army, I'll study about that too."

Well, Robin and about half his men agreed and went with the King, but the rest of 'em said they had got so they liked that life out there in the woods best, and so they stayed.

"Do you remember who it was you heard tell that tale, Uncle Kel?" I asked.

"Heard it when I was a boy. Ain't thought of it for more'n thirty years. My father told it as far as I can recollect. He knowed a sight of old tales — songs, too."

"Did you ever hear a *song* about Robin Hood?"

"Why!" said Delia, "Norah Harmon, lives over on the road to Stanley, she knows a song about the two fellers bein' rescued from the sheriff. Hit's just the same as the tale, but it rhymes out real good and she's got a tune to it."

"I know a tale!" said ten-year-old Stan. "Boy in my room told it the other day. Said his mommy learned it to him. Teacher always lets us tell tales last thing on a Friday — if we been good all week."

And without much urging Stan plunged in a bit breathlessly.

SODY SALLYRAYTUS

One time there was an old woman and an old man and a little girl and a little boy — and a pet squirrel sittin' up on the fireboard. And one day the old woman wanted to bake some biscuits but she didn't have no sody, so she sent the little boy off to the store for some sody sallyraytus. The little boy he went trottin' on down the road singin', "Sody, sody, sody sallyraytus!" Trotted across the bridge and on to the store and got the sody sallyraytus, and started trottin' on back.

Got to the bridge and started across and an old bear stuck his head out from under it, says:

"I'LL EAT YOU UP — YOU AND YOUR SODY SALLYRAYTUS!"

So he swallered the little boy — him and his sody sallyraytus.

The old woman and the old man and the little girl and the pet squirrel they waited and they waited for the little boy, but he didn't come and didn't come, so fin'lly the old woman sent the little girl after the little boy. She skipped down the road and skipped across the bridge and on to the store, and the storekeeper told her the little boy had already been there and gone. So she started skippin' back, and when she got to the bridge the old bear stuck his head out—

"I EAT A LITTLE BOY, HIM AND HIS SODY SALLYRAYTUS —AND I'LL EAT YOU TOO!"

So he swallered her down.

The old woman and the old man and the pet squirrel they waited and waited but the little girl didn't come and didn't come, so the old woman sent the old man after the little boy and the little girl. He walked on down the road, walked across the bridge—*Karump! Karump! Karump!*—and walked on till he came to the store, and the storekeeper told him the little boy and the little girl had already been there and gone.

"They must'a stopped somewhere 'side the road to play."

So the old man he started walkin' on back. Got to the bridge—

"I EAT A LITTLE BOY, HIM AND HIS SODY SALLYRAYTUS, AND I EAT A LITTLE GIRL—AND I'LL EAT YOU, TOO!"

And the old bear reached and grabbed the old man and swallered him.

Well, the old woman and the pet squirrel they waited and waited but the old man didn't come and didn't come. So the old woman *she* put out a-hunchety-hunchin' down the road, crossed the bridge, got to the store, and the storekeeper told her, says, "That boy's already done been here and gone—him and the little girl and the old man, too."

So the old woman she went hunchin' on back—a-hunchety-hunchety-hunch. Got to the bridge—

"I EAT A LITTLE BOY, HIM AND HIS SODY SALLYRAYTUS, AND I EAT A LITTLE GIRL, AND I EAT AN OLD MAN—AND I'LL EAT YOU, TOO!"

Reached out and grabbed her, and swallered *her* up.

Well, the pet squirrel he waited and he waited and he waited, and he went to runnin' back and forth up there on the fireboard, and he was gettin' hungrier and hungrier; so fin'lly he jumped down on the table, jumped off on the bench, and jumped to the floor. Shook his tail out behind him and out the door and down the road, just a-friskin'. Scuttered across the bridge and on in the store. R'ared up on his hindquarters and looked for the storekeeper, squarked a time or two, and when the storekeeper looked and saw him, the pet squirrel raised up on his tiptoes and asked him had he seen anything of the little boy or the little girl or the old man or the old woman.

"Law, yes! They all done already been here and gone. Surely they ain't *all* done stopped 'side the road to play."

So the pet squirrel he stretched his tail out behind him and frisked out the door. Frisked on over the bridge—

"I EAT A LITTLE BOY, HIM AND HIS SODY SALLYRAYTUS, AND I EAT A LITTLE GIRL, AND I EAT AN OLD MAN, AND I EAT AN OLD WOMAN—AND I'LL EAT YOU, TOO!"

The little pet squirrel he stuck his tail straight up in the air and just chittered, but time the old bear made for him he was already scratchin' halfway up a tree. The old bear he went clamberin' up to get him. The squirrel got 'way out on a limb, and the old bear started out the limb after him. The squirrel he jumped and caught in the next tree.

"HUMPF! IF YOU CAN MAKE IT WITH YOUR LITTLE LEGS, I *KNOW* I CAN MAKE IT WITH MY BIG 'UNS!"

And the old bear tried to jump—didn't quite make it. Down he went and when he hit the ground he split wide open.

The old woman stepped out, and the old man he stepped out, and the little girl jumped out, and the little boy he jumped out. And the old woman says, "Where's my sody sallyraytus?"

"Here," says the little boy, and he handed it to her.

So they went on back to the house and the pet squirrel he scooted on ahead of 'em, cloomb back up on the fireboard and curled his tail over his back, and watched the old woman till she took the biscuits out the oven. So then she broke him off a chunk and blew on it till it wasn't too hot, and handed it up to him. And he took it in his forepaws and turned it over and over and nibbled on it—and when he eat it up he leaned down and chittered for some more. And he was so hungry the old woman had to hand him chunks till he'd eat two whole biscuits.

"Why, that's like one I read in a book!" exclaimed one of the girls.

"Billy Goats Gruff," snorted one of the boys. "I read that in the third grade, but it wasn't like that; didn't have no squirrel in it nor no bear."

"Did ye ever hear about the old sow and her three shoats?" asked Old Rob. "That's in your books, too. Hit was even in the picture show down at Newton here a few months back."

"Law me!" said Granny. "Have they done gone and put that old tale in the movin' pictures?"

"They called it 'The Three Little Pigs,' but it wasn't the way you told it to us."

"Tell it, Granny!" came from all sides —

"Let Big Rob tell it." She chuckled. "Hit's one of your Jack-'n-Will-'n-Tom tales."

Old Rob gave the two children on his lap a jounce and started out —

THE OLD SOW AND
THE THREE SHOATS

One time there was an old sow lived 'way out in the woods under a rock-clift, had three little shoats. One was named Will, he was the oldest; and the next 'un was Tom, and the least 'un was named Jack. Well, them little shoats thought it was time they went out to seek their fortune and the old sow told 'em, says, "When you build you a house build it out of rocks and bricks so the old red fox can't get ye. And come back to visit your old mammy every Sunday."

Well, Will, he started out first. The old sow fixed him three days' rations and a little house-plunder on a drag-sled and he went on out in the wilderness, and directly he met the old red fox.

"Hello, little piggy! Where ye started?"

"Started out to build me a house."

"What you goin' to build it out'n?"

"Rocks and bricks."

"Oo, no, little piggy! Rocks and bricks'll be awful cold. Why, you 'uld freeze! Build your house out of chips and cornstalks."

So Will he built his house out of chips and cornstalks, and that night the old red fox come to the door.

"Hello, little piggy! Let me in so I can warm."

"Oh, no! I'm feared you might eat me up!"

> "By the beard on my chin,
> I'll blow your house in!"

So the old red fox he r'ared back on his hindquarters and blowed — blowed the house over and grabbed Will and eat him up.

And Will didn't come back to see his old mammy that Sunday.

Well, pretty soon Tom started out. The old sow fixed him up three days' rations and a little house-plunder on a drag-sled and he went on out in the wilderness. Met the old red fox.

"Hello, little piggy! Where ye started to?"

"Goin' to build me a house."

"What ye goin' to build it out'n?"

"Rocks and bricks!"

"Oo-oo, no, little piggy! That'll freeze ye. Build it outa chips and cornstalks."

So Tom he got to studyin' about it and he 'lowed it 'uld be a heap easier to build him a house outa chips and cornstalks anyhow, so that's what he done.

And that night the old red fox came to the door.

"Let me in, little piggy, so I can warm."

"Oh, no! I'm feared you'll eat me up."

> "By the beard on my chin,
> I'll blow your house in!"

So the old red fox he r'ared back on his hindquarters and blowed — blowed that house all to pieces and grabbed Tom and eat him up.

And so Tom failed to show up at his mammy's that Sunday.

Fin'lly the old sow she fixed Jack three days' rations and a little house-plunder on a drag-sled and he headed for the wilderness. Met up with the old red fox.

"Hello there, little piggy! Where ye started?"

"Started out to seek my fortune. Goin' to build me a house."

"What ye goin' to build it out'n?"

"Build it outa rocks 'n bricks."

"Oo-oo-oo no, little piggy! Don't build it outa rocks 'n bricks. Why, you'd plumb freeze! You ought to build your house outa chips and cornstalks so you'll be warm."

But Jack went on and done what his mammy told him. Cleared him a tract and built him a good house outa rocks and bricks. Built up a big fire in the fireplace and put on a potful of peas for his supper.

And that night here came the old red fox.

"Oh, little piggy, let me in so I can warm."

"Oh, no! You'd eat me up!"

> *"By the beard on my chin,*
> *I'll blow your house in!"*

"Go ahead and blow," says Jack.

So the old red fox he blowed and blowed and blowed and blowed till he give out, but he couldn't blow Jack's house down.

So directly he went around to the back door and commenced whinin', says, "Oo-oo, little piggy, I'm a-freezin'! Just let me put my nose in and get hit warm."

"Oh, no," says Jack, "I'm afraid you might nose me out."

The old red fox he kept on beggin' Jack to open the door just enough to let his nose in till Jack he opened the door a little crack and the old red fox stuck his nose in. Jack mashed the door back hard on his nose, and the old red fox says, "Oo-oo, little piggy,

how good that fire smells! Just let me put my paws in and get them warm, too."

"Oh, no! I'm afraid you'd paw me out."

Kept on beggin', Jack let his paws in, mashed the door back.

"Oo-oo, little piggy, my shoulders is freezin'! Just let my shoulders in."

"'Fraid you'd shoulder me out!"

Fin'lly Jack let his shoulders in. Mashed the door back, nearly pinched the old red fox in two.

"Oo-oo! That's nice and warm, little piggy, but my rump is freezin'."

"Oh, no, you'd rump me out."

Begged and begged, so Jack let the old red fox in all but his tail. Slammed the door back and held him by the tail.

"Oo-oo, little piggy! My tail is freezin' plumb off. Please do just let my tail in, little piggy. I'll go on out ag'in jest as soon as I get warmed up good."

So Jack eased up on the door and then the old red fox was in, all of him. He went over and laid up in the fireplace, commenced mumblin' and hummin' and kept lookin' over there at Jack with his jaws just a-drippin'. Jack went on about his business, and directly he heard what he was a-singin', says:

> "Bakebilly boo!
> Bakebilly boo!
> Pig and peas for supper!
> Pig and peas!"

So Jack threw up his head like he heard somethin' outside, run to the door and looked out.

"What ye see, little piggy?"

"Oh, it ain't nothin'," says Jack, "'cept the King comin' with all his pack of foxhounds."

"O law!" says the old red fox, "I better hide quick! Where'll I hide, little piggy? Where'll I hide?"

"Jump in that churn there," says Jack. "I'll not tell where you're at."

So the old red fox he jumped in the churn, and Jack nailed the churn lid down, stuck a kettle of water on the pothook.

The old red fox kept right still and Jack he't that water scaldin' hot. Then he took it off the fire and commenced pourin' it in the hole in the churn-lid.

"Oo-oo-oo!" says the old fox. "A little more cold, little piggy! Just a little more cold!"

But Jack he kept puttin' it to him scaldin' hot and the old red fox fin'lly fluttered his tail — wh-r-r-r-r! flop! flop! flop! — and that was the end of him.

So Jack pulled out the nails and poured the old red fox out the back door, and rinsed the churn. Then he eat his pot of peas for supper and went on to bed.

And Jack lived right on in his house and nothin' never bothered him, and he went back to see his old mammy every Sunday.

"Tom," said Jeems, "what was that tale we mentioned almost first thing when we got here? Had the devil in it. If Rob hadn't told 'Wicked John' I could think what it was."

"Bobtail?"

"That's it."

"'That beats Bobtail, and Bobtail beat the Devil,'" I quoted. "Is that a tale?"

"That's the byword," said Tom. "The tale's about how Bobtail done it. I reckon the tale got the byword started."

And before the boys could say "Tell it! Tell it!" Tom had started —

HOW BOBTAIL
BEAT THE DEVIL

One time the Devil he decided he'd like to try a little farmin'. The climate wasn't much good for it down there where he lived at, so he come up here and went to lookin' around. First man he run across was Bobtail. Now if the old Devil had-a knowed how hard Bobtail was to beat in a trade he might-a waited till the next feller come along. Anyhow, there was Bobtail walkin' in home. So the Devil he stepped up beside him and commenced talkin' while they ambled on down the road.

"You live around here?"

"Um-humh."

"You a farmer?"

"Um-humh."

"I been thinkin' about goin' into farmin' myself."

"Say ye have?"

"I'm a-lookin' for me a partner."

"Ye are?"

"How would you like to do a little share-croppin' with me?"

"I might," says Bobtail. — The Devil had his hat pulled 'way down over his forehead but Bobtail had done noticed two little sharp-like bumps a-pushin' out the felt; seen one of his feet was too big, didn't have nothin' in the shoe-toe, looked like it was all in the ankle. — So Bobtail asked him, says, "What share of the crop do you want, mister?"

"Why, I don't hardly know now," says the Devil. "Jest what do ye mean?"

"Do you gener'lly take what grows above ground or what grows below?"

The Devil told him, says, "Oh, I always take what grows above ground."

So Bobtail and him put in a crop. And when it got ripe and they went to gather it, the Devil he cut off the tops and stacked 'em up real careful; and then Bobtail he got his bull-tongue plow and his grabbler and pretty soon there was his potatoes. So he put 'em in the cellar. And the Devil he took a load of his part of the crop to town and asked around about potato tops, and it didn't take him long to find out he'd been cheated. Got back in, says, "Bobtail, next time *I'm* to have what grows below the ground."

So the next season the Devil come back, and Bobtail put him to work: plowin', harrerin', plantin', choppin' — made the old Devil sweat. And when that crop got ripe Bobtail says to him, says, "Well, I'll clean off the top of the ground for you this time." So he cut the corn and shocked it in the orchard; handed the Devil a mattick, says, "Here." — And they tell me the old Devil grubbed up every corn-root in the field; washed a few of 'em, put 'em in a bushel basket and carried 'em on to town. Come back after a while, says, "Bobtail, let's us try some other kind of farmin'."

Bobtail asked him how about pigs, and the Devil said all right; so they got some brood-sows and the sows they found little pigs directly, and it wasn't long till the shoats was runnin' all over the place. They kept feedin' 'em corn — the Devil had to buy his corn — and them pigs growed till pretty soon they got to weighin' around eighteen-nineteen hundred pounds — like the pigs we raised when I was a boy. And one day the Devil come, says, "Bobtail, ain't it about time we divided up them pigs?"

"Yes, I reckon they're about big enough by now," says Bobtail.

"How'll we get 'em divided out?" the Devil asked him.

"Why, I don't know," says Bobtail. "Can you count?"

"Why, no, I can't count. Can't you count?"

"No," says Bobtail, "I never was much of a hand with figgers."

"Well, how'n the nation can we divide them pigs?" the Devil asked him.

"Tell ye what," Bobtail says to him, "if it's all right with you: see that field there next to this 'un, and that rail fence runnin' down the middle of it from yonder side the pig-lot — makes two fields over there? Now, you can throw a pig in one field, and then I'll throw one in the other field; then you throw another'n and I'll throw me one — and that way we'll not have much bother gettin' the pigs divided up."

Well, the Devil he went to that side of the pig-lot, looked down the fence a ways; come back, says, "Why, yes, I reckon that'll be all right."

"You can have the first throw," Bobtail told him. Says, "Wait just a minute." And he went and got him a couple of bushels of corn, dumped it in the middle of his field. Come on back, says, "Go ahead; you throw first now."

So the Devil he picked out the biggest, fattest sow in the lot, pitched her over, turned back around quick and looked and looked to see which was the next biggest 'un. Then Bobtail tackled him one, only a fairly big 'un, dragged her to the fence by her ears, got under her and heaved, and fin'lly over she went. The Devil had done grabbed him another great big hog by the hind leg, so he flipped it over; and Bobtail he wrestled with his next 'un till he got

hit over. And they kept on pitchin' out pigs till there wasn't but one left—and it was the Devil's turn to throw. He thought he had Bobtail sure on this trade 'cause that made the extra pig his'n. So he got it cornered and picked it up, dropped it over; and then he looked over in the field—and there wasn't a pig in sight but that last 'un, and he seen it run down to where there was a couple of rails rotted out, scrouge under the fence and run a-squealin' to Bobtail's pile of corn.

"Look a-yonder, Bobtail! All my pigs have done gone and got mixed up with your'n!"

"That don't differ none," Bobtail told him. Says, "I'll know *my* pigs."

"How?" the Devil wanted to know.

"Why," says Bobtail, "ever' pig I threw out I reached down just 'fore I let go of it and twisted its tail right hard—left it in a curl."

And they say the old Devil spent the rest of the day over there amongst all them pigs, tryin' to find the ones that had straight tails.

But the Devil he studied up a way he thought he could surely outdo Bobtail. Come to him directly, says, "Bobtail, let's you and me play pitchhammer a couple of rounds. I got a real good hammer for pitchin'. I'll go down yonder and get it."

Well, he got the hammer and they went out in the bottom fields to play. The Devil he whirled it around and around, let go of it — and straight up it went. Shot through a couple of clouds, went past two or three more — went on up out of sight. Bobtail kept lookin' up for it to fall; and the Devil let him look a while. Then he says to him, says, "I'll jest tell ye, Bobtail: there ain't no use waitin' for it. Hit'll not fall till tomorrer sometime."

So they went on to the house and fooled around; and jest 'fore dinner the next day they heard it hit — WHAM! "Come on," says the Devil. So they went back down to the bottom pasture; and sure enough, there was that hammer mired in the ground about half-way up the handle. The Devil he pulled it out and laid it down. Stepped back, says, "All right, Bobtail."

So Bobtail went to look the hammer over. Walked up the handle, walked around the head, and here he come walkin' back down the other side the handle. The Devil had one hand in his pocket and was r'ared back jest a-grinnin'. Well, Bobtail he took his stand at the end of the handle; then he looked away up in the sky, put his hands up to his mouth, hollered, "Hey, Saint Peter! Open the gate and move back out the way! — Gabriel! You better move over to one side! — You little angels now, you run back and stand right close to the throne. Some of ye might get hurt." And Bobtail he bent down like he was goin' to grab holt on the Devil's hammer.

The old Devil come over there quick. "Un-unh, Bobtail! I didn't know you was aimin' to pitch my hammer *that* high! Why, if you was to throw my hammer up in that place, I never would get it back. Jest let it alone now and let me have it."

So the Devil took his hammer and went on back where he come from, and he ain't been seen in that part of the country since.

"Aaa Lord!" roared Old Rob. "Tom, you've done beat Bobtail and the Devil, too! I hadn't never heard but the first part of that. — 'Hey, Saint Peter! Watch out now!'" — and the old man fairly bounced with mirth. "That puts me in mind of a song. — Here, Rhody, these young'uns have done gone to sleep on me. Take 'em and lay 'em on the bed."

Rhody and Steve carried the two little girls and stretched them out on the far side of the big bed where they whimpered a time or two, curled up and slept again.

Tom got up and tended the fire. Steve brought another stick and laid it in place. Two big boys who had been standing against the wall, moved and sat down on the floor leaning on each other back-to-back.

"What was that song Bobtail put you in mind of?" asked Jeems.

"Don't you sing that old thing," protested Sarah. "We done had enough devilment already."

"She don't like it," said little Rob, "'cause it throws off on woman-kind."

A chorus of "Sing it! Go on, sing it!" came from the big boys; and Old Robin sang —

The Devil and the Farmer's Wife

There was an old man at the foot of the hill:
if he ain't moved a-way he's living there still.
Sing high diddle I, diddle I fy,
diddle I, diddle I, day!
Now this old man in Ohio did dwell;
he had an old woman he wished her — well.
So the Devil he came to his house one day,
says, "One of your family I'm a-goin' to take away."
"O please don't take my oldest son;
there's work on the farm that's got to be done."
"It's neither your son nor your daughter I crave
but your old scolding woman I now must have."

THE DEVIL AND THE FARMER'S WIFE

There was an old man at the foot of the hill:

if he ain't moved a-way he's livin' there still.

Sing high diddle I, diddle I fy,

diddle I, diddle I, day!

"Take her on, take her on, with the joy of my heart!
I hope, by golly, you'll nevermore part."
So the Devil he bundled her up in a sack
and slung her up across his back.
He carried her down to the high gates of hell,
says, "Punch up the fire, we're goin' to roast her well."
In come a little devil draggin' his chains;
she jerked off her slipper and beat out his brains.
Twelve little devils went a-climbin' up higher;
she up with her foot, kicked eleven in the fire.
The odd little devil peeped over the wall,
says, "Take her back, Daddy! She'll murder us all!"
Now that old man was a peekin' through a crack;
he seen the poor Devil a-waggin' her back.
The old man run and hid under the bed;
she up with the butterstick and battered his head.
And now you see what a woman can do:
she can outdo her husband and the Devil too.

Old Kel roared even louder than Big Rob did over Bobtail, especially at the verse, "Take her back, Daddy!" and two of the boys
on the floor listening open-mouthed while each verse came out
in Rob's big voice, cut all kinds of antics in their glee at the end
of every punch line. Tom spoke out above their hilarity, "You boys
might get in a little more dry wood; that green log's about to
smother the fire."

All the boys trailed out to the woodpile. There was general going
in and out for a few minutes; drinks of water from the cedar bucket
in the kitchen, wood brought and the fire mended, more wood
toted in and piled on one end of the hearthrock. Three sleepy
smaller children were bundled up to be taken down the road a
piece by a pair of boys who urged that no tales be told in their ab-
sence. Tom had been whetting his knife on a pocket-stone in the

course of the last three or four tales, and now he was whittling on a small block of wood.

"You whittlin' somethin'," asked Steve, "or just a-whittlin' whittlin's?"

"Somethin'," said Tom. "You'll see."

"You doin' much for that guild outfit?" asked Jeems.

"Crosses, puzzle balls, bears; dog or cat now and then."

"What's that about a guild?" I asked.

"Craft guild," said Jeems. "Episcopal Church started it about ten years ago. It helps folks in here sell little pretties they make: wood-carvin', weavin', cornshuck dolls, all kinds of oldtime crafts and toys. Show him some of your stuff, Tom."

Tom brought a carton full of little carved and polished crosses strung on black ribbon, figures of sturdy bears, barking dogs, archback cats, and a handful of "puzzle balls" — six little bars of slotted wood rounded on each end and fitted together into a sphere. Steve took one apart and challenged me to reassemble it. I took it, and managed to match the slots after a few fumbles.

The boys were intent on what Tom was carving.

"You ain't never made anything like that before, have ye?" asked Steve.

"Just remembered this trick here the other day. My grandpa used to make 'em. I tried one yesterday but I made a bobble of it. Think I can get it right this time."

"What's it goin' to be?" insisted Stan.

"You'll see. You just wait now till I get it done."

The boys who'd had to take the kids home stomped back in the house. "Hit's done clouded over," one of them announced; "not a star showin'." They held their hands at the newly wakened fire, and then sat down on the floor with their feet thrust toward the warmth. "We ain't missed no tales, have we?"

About Nine-Thirty . . .

"I been tryin' to get my mind on a tale," said Old Rob, "while you was all lookin' at Tom's play-pretties. Hit was about a preacher named Dry Guy, or somethin'. Dad, you told it one day when I was helpin' you cut timber over in the head of Morning Star holler; must 'a been ten years back. We was eatin' our grub, and you was sittin' on a big flat rock and I'd took my dinner-bucket and got propped up against a big poplar — and you told that tale. I can remember it like yesterday — all but the tale. Everybody had to get shet of the old preacher somehow, and — "

"'Old Dry Frye'?"

"That's the very one! Tell it again."

Old Kel had been crumbling tobacco in the palm of his hand, and now he scooped it up and tamped it into a little store-bought cob pipe, and pondered, mumbling something about "can't recollect all of it just right — one part there I can't get . . ."

Stan broke off a dry splinter from a stick of firewood, lit it, and held it to Uncle Kel's pipe.

"Well, I'll try to get it started and it'll come out all right, I reckon. I'll put it together some way or other."

OLD DRY FRYE

One time there was an old man named Dry Frye. He was a
preacher but all he preached for was revival collections and
all the fried chicken he could eat. And one time he stayed for
supper and he was eatin' fried chicken so fast he got a chicken
bone stuck in his throat. Choked him to death. Well, the man of
the house he was scared. "Law me!" he says, "they'll find old Dry
Frye here and they'll hang me for murder sure!" So he took old
Dry Frye to a house down the road a piece and propped him up
against the door. Somebody went to go out the door directly old
Dry Frye fell in the house. "Law me!" says the man of the house.
"Hit's old Dry Frye!" (Everybody knew old Dry Frye.) "We got to
get shet of him quick or we're liable to be hung for murder!"

So he took old Dry Frye and propped him up in the bresh 'side
the road. And way up in the night some men come along, thought
it was a highway robber layin' for 'em. So they chunked rocks at
him, knocked him down, and when they seen who it was (every-

body knew old Dry Frye) they thought they'd killed him, and they got scared they'd be hung for murder 'cause they'd passed several people on the road who'd 'a knowed who was along there that night.

Well, they took old Dry Frye and propped him up against a man's cornhouse. And that man he went out early the next mornin'; and he'd been missin' corn — so when he seen there was somebody over there at his cornhouse he ran and got his gun. Slipped around, hollered, "Get away from there or I'll shoot!"

And when old Dry Frye never moved he shot and Dry Frye tumbled over and hit the ground.

"Law me!" says the man. "I believe that was old Dry Frye." (Everybody knew old Dry Frye.) "Now I've done killed him and I'll sure get hung for murder."

So he went and saw it *was* him and seen how dead he was, and went to studyin' up some way to get shet of him. Well, he throwed him in the cornhouse to hide him, and that night he took old Dry Frye down to a baptizin' place 'side a bend in the river where they were fixin' to have a big baptizin' the next day, propped him up on a stump on the riverbank — over a right deep place where the bank was pretty high — propped his elbows on his knees and his chin in his hands. Made him look awful natural. Left him there, went on home and slept sound.

So early the next mornin', 'fore anybody else, a little old feisty boy came down there foolin' around the baptizin' place. Saw old Dry Frye, hollered, "Howdy, Mr. Frye."

Went over closer.

"Howdy, Mr. Dry Frye."

Old Dry Frye sat right on.

"I said Howdy, Dry Frye."

Old Dry Frye kept on sittin'. That boy, now he was just as feisty as he could be. He didn't care how he spoke to nobody.

"Look-a-here, Old Dry Frye, if you don't answer me Howdy I'm goin' to knock your elbows out from under you. — Howdy, Mr. Frye!"

So that feisty boy he reached over and swiped old Dry Frye a lick and over in the river the old man went, right down the bank into that deep water, sunk clean out of sight. Then that boy thought sure he'd drownded Dry Frye. He got scared about bein' hung for murder but he couldn't do nothin' about it right then 'cause he'd seen folks comin' down the road for the baptizin'. So he hung around and directly everybody gathered for the baptizin', and they waited and waited for old Dry Frye to come and preach, but he didn't come and didn't come and when they got to askin' who'd seen old Dry Frye, one man said he'd left his place right after supper, and another man said why, no, he'd not seen old Dry Frye since last meetin'. And that feisty boy he 'uld let out a giggle where he was sittin' on one of the benches in the back, and the other boys 'uld ask him what he was laughin' at but he'd just get tickled again and not tell 'em nothin'. So fin'lly the folks sung a few hymns and took up a collection. So meetin' broke and everybody went on home, and that boy he went on home, too.

Then 'way along late that night he went down and hooked old Dry Frye out of the river and put him in a sack. Got his shoulder under it and started down the road to hide him somewhere. Well, there were a couple of rogues comin' along that same night, had stole a couple of hogs and had 'em sacked up carryin' 'em on their shoulders. Them rogues came over a little rise in the road, saw that boy and they got scared, dropped their sacks and run back lickety-split and hid in the bresh. The boy he never saw the two rogues so he came on, saw them two sacks and set old Dry Frye down to see what was in the other sacks. Then he left old Dry Frye layin' there, picked up one of the hogs and went on back home.

So the two rogues they slipped out directly and when they saw the two sacks still layin' there, they picked 'em up and kept on goin'. Got in home and hung the sacks up in the meathouse. Then the next mornin' the old woman got up to cook breakfast, went out to the smokehouse to cut some meat. Ripped open one of them sacks and there hung old Dry Frye. Well, she hollered and dropped her butcher knife and she got away from there in such a hurry she tore down one side of the smokehouse, broke out two posts on the back porch, and knocked the kitchen door clean off the hinges. She was sorta scared. She hollered and squalled and the men come runnin' in their shirt-tails and fin'lly looked out in the smokehouse, saw old Dry Frye hangin' up there in the place of a hog.

"Law me!" says one of 'em. "Hit's old Dry Frye!" (Everybody knew old Dry Frye.) "We'll sure be hung for murder if we don't get shet of him some way or other."

Well, they had some wild horses in a wilderness out on the mountain. So they rounded up one of 'em, got him in the barn. Then they put an old no-'count saddle on him and an old piece of bridle, and put old Dry Frye on. Stropped his legs to the bellyband, tied his hands to the saddlehorn and pulled the reins through, stuck his old hat on his head; and then they slipped out and opened all the gates. Opened the barn door and let the horse go. He shot out of there and down the road he went with that old preacher-man a-bouncin' first one side and then the other. And them rogues run out and went to shootin' and hollerin', "He's stole our horse! Stop him! Somebody stop him yonder! Horse thief! Horse thief!" Everybody down the road come runnin' out their houses a-shoutin' and hollerin' and a-shootin' around, but that horse had done jumped the fence and took out up the mountain and it looked like he was headed for Kentucky.

And as far as I know old Dry Frye is over there yet a-tearin' around through the wilderness on that wild horse.

"Rhody," said Granny, "did I ever tell you about Catskins?"

"No, ma'am."

"You girls'll like this one," said Delia.

Granny London clasped her thin hands together over her knee and leaned forward . . .

Rhody's boyish restlessness seemed to leave her as the tale unfolded. She listened breathlessly, her eyes dreaming with a quiet intensity as Granny evoked the ancient spell — the fate of the beautiful young girl who once, in ages past, had to play her part sitting in the ashes . . .

CATSKINS

Once there was a girl had no father and mother. She stayed with some people and they made her work for what she ate. They never paid her a thing, didn't give her any clothes or nothin'. All she had was one old dress, and when it got ragged all she could find to patch it with was old cat-hides; and fin'lly her whole dress wasn't nothin' but cat-skins — cat-skins all over, with the tails hangin' out. So they called her Catskins.

Well, this man's wife she took sick and died. And one day, fairly soon after the buryin', the man was out in the fields plowin'; and Catskins she washed herself and put on the dead woman's weddin' dress: went out in the yard and started walkin' around. That man he saw her and came runnin' to the house. He looked at Catskins and asked her would she marry him.

"Well," she says, "you get me a dress the color of all the fish that swim in the sea."

So he got her the dress. Said, "Will you marry me now?"

She says to him, says, "Will you get me a dress the color of all the birds that fly through the air?"

He got her that kind of a dress, says, "Will you marry me?"

"Now," she says to him, "you'll have to get me a dress the color of all the flowers that grow in the world."

So he went and got her that dress, says, "Now will you marry me?"

"I might marry ye," she told him, "if you give me your flyin' box."

He didn't want to part with his flyin' box, but he wanted to marry Catskins awful bad; so he went and got her the flyin' box. — "Now, let's get married."

"Well," she says, "you go on out so I can put on one of my dresses."

And time the man left out the back door Catskins dragged the flyin' box out the front door, put all her dresses in it; then she got in the box right quick, says:

> "Rise and fly!
> 'Way up high!'"

And the box rose up in the air and Catskins flew on off from there.

She flew right on across the country till she saw a big house—

> "Light me down!
> Right to the ground!'"

The box lit, and she got out—

> "Sink and lock,
> under this rock!'"

So the box sunk out of sight under the rock, and Catskins she went on to the big house in her old cat-skin dress. It was a rich man lived there, and Catskins went around to the back door and knocked. The woman of the house opened the door and looked out; and when she saw Catskins, she jumped.

"Law me! What do you want?"

"I want to work."

"Do you think I'd hire a thing like you?"

The old woman's girl was standin' there by the door, says, "Don't be so hard-hearted, Mother. Let her work in the kitchen."

"All right then — but never a bite she cooks will go in *my* mouth."

So Catskins went to the kitchen to go to work; and time she walked in the door with them cats' tails a-hangin' out all over her, the kitchen folks was scared to death. They ran out of there like somethin' was after 'em! Then some of 'em slipped back and peeked around the doors, and hollered "Scat!" But when they saw it was just a poor girl and not any sort of varmint they came on back; and so Catskins went to work with the poor folks there in the kitchen.

Well, they were havin' a big dance at the King's house one night and Catskins was helpin' that girl get ready to go.

"You want to go, Catskins? You can look in the windows with the other poor folks."

Catskins said she didn't think she'd go: she might — and she might not. Then when they'd all left, she went to her box —

"Rise again,
and let me in!"

And the box rose from under the rock and unlocked itself for her. She took out the dress that was the color of all the fish in the sea and put it on and got in her box and flew on up to the King's house.

"Who's that?" everybody said when she walked in. "Who can that be?" But nobody knew who she was.

The King's son was there and he took off with her right now! Kept her for his partner and they led off in every set they danced. That boy he kept his eyes on Catskins every minute but she hardly let him talk to her; and directly they were doin' Lady-'Round-the-Lady, and she and that boy got around the set to the couple near the door, and when Catskins did Lady-'Round-the-Gent-and-the-Gent-Don't-Go she slipped out the door and ran to her box and flew on back. And when they all came home there she was sittin' by the kitchen fire in her old cat-skin dress.

"Were you there, Catskins?"

"Yes, I was there."

"Did you see that pretty girl?"

"Yes, I saw her."

"Well, the King is havin' another dance tonight. I wonder will that girl come." Said, "You let me sleep till three o'clock tomorrow; I want to be beautiful for that dance."

So the next night Catskins helped that girl get her hair done up, and after they all left she went to her box. And when she walked in that time she had on her dress the color of all the birds in the air.

"There she is!" they all went to whisperin'. "That's her!" But nobody knew who she was.

The King's son he got her again and they danced and she talked to him a little. She had a hard time gettin' away from him because he wouldn't pay attention to anybody but her — but fin'lly she slipped out the door and took off; and when they all got back to the house there was little old Catskins sittin' in the kitchen.

"O Catskins! Were you there?"

"Yes, I was there."

"And did you see what a pretty dress that girl had on this time?"

"Yes, I saw it."

"They say the King's boy is struck on her — hard. He's goin' to have another dance tomorrow night. Don't you wake me up till four o'clock. I want to be real beautiful, because this is the last dance."

Well, the next night the girl said to Catskins, "If you want to go, I'll lend you one of my dresses, and you can come on in and dance."

"Humpf!" said the old woman. "You can lend her a dress if you want to, but never a dress of *mine* will go on her back!"

So the girl got one of her old dresses for Catskins, and Catskins thanked her and when they'd all left she went to her box and got out her dress the color of all the flowers in the world. And when she walked in the King's house that time everybody just carried on over how beautiful she was, and they all tried to figure out who she could be, but nobody knew her.

The King's boy wouldn't let go of her hand all evenin', and they danced and danced — every figure, from Four-Hands-Round to Killiecrankie — and she talked to him, and they laughed, and everybody had the best kind of time. Then, just about midnight, he slipped a ring on her finger and when he did that he let go of her hand a second, and Catskins was out the door and gone 'fore he could turn around.

So she hid her dresses and that ring in the flyin' box and made it hide again under that rock—and when they all came back in home there was little Catskins sittin' in the kitchen up against the fire place with soot and ashes all over her face and hands.

"Oo, Catskins! Were you there tonight?"

"Yes, I was there."

"Why, I never saw ye."

"I saw you."

"Well, did you ever see such a pretty dress as that girl had on?"

"Yes, it was right pretty."

"Well, there won't be any more dances now; and they say that when that girl left nobody saw which way she went or nothin'. And they tell me the King's boy never did learn her name or where she came from."

The very next day the King's son started huntin' for the girl who wore the three beautiful dresses. He hunted and he searched, and he asked everybody he met up with but nobody could tell him a thing; but he kept on searchin' and huntin' for her, and he wouldn't eat, and fin'lly he was sick-in-bed. The doctors came and they said he was lovesick: said he'd die unless that girl was found.

Well, all the girls tried to make up to him; baked him cakes and took 'em up there to where he was lyin' sick-in-bed. So one day Catskins said she'd bake a cake for him.

"I say!" That old woman went to squawkin'. "*You* bake him a cake! He *would* get sick if *you* was to bake him a cake!"

"Aw, Mother, don't be so hard-hearted. Let her bake him a cake if she wants to."

"Well! There'll be no bite of it go in *my* mouth!"

So Catskins she went and got that ring, and when she baked

the cake she put the ring in it. She got it baked and made it real pretty with white icin', and then the old woman she came and took it away from her.

"You ugly thing! Do you think you could go up there in your old cat-hides? I'll take it to him myself."

So she traipsed on up to the King's house, and took the cake on in to that boy. His mother cut him a piece and that ring fell out on the plate.

"Why, look!" she says. "It's a ring!"

And when she showed it to that boy he sat up, says, "Where did that ring come from?"

"Out of the cake."

"Who baked it?"

"I did," said the old woman. "I did!"

"No such thing!" the King's son told her. "Whoever baked that cake you bring her here right now, or I'll have your head cut off!" And he called for his clothes and started gettin' up out the bed.

The old woman she left there scared to death, and she fetched Catskins back in a hurry.

Catskins stood there in the door and the King's son looked at her, and then she smiled.

"You're the very one!" he said; and he went to take her by the hand, but she turned and ran out again. She went and raised her box, and then she got in it—

> *"Rise and fly!*
> *Not too high!"*

And it rose up and took her back to the King's place. She put on the first dress and came in the house.

The King's son looked at her, says, "No—the other one."

So she went and came back in with the second dress on.

"No—that's not right yet."

She went and put on her flower dress and when she came back in that time he went to her and took her hands and kissed her.

"Will you marry me?"

"Yes," Catskins told him.

So they got married, and they lived happy.

And some folks tell it that the King made that old woman put on the catskin dress and work in his kitchen the rest of her days.

A man had come to the door about the time the tale was well started. He rapped once and pushed the door open. "You kids come on home." Several children got up.

"Stay a while, Harry," said Tom. "Let Granny finish this tale for 'em."

Harry had come in and found a seat.

"That tale," said Tom, "is like Ashpet — one my wife knew." And Tom Hunt kept on slicing and digging and flicking chips with his knife as he started telling his tale. The father who had come for his children made no move to go.

ASHPET

One time there was a woman had two daughters, and they kept a hired girl. They treated this girl mean. She was bound out to 'em, had to do all the hard work, little as she was. They wouldn't buy her any pretty clothes or nothin', made her sleep right up against the fireplace and the ashes got all over her, so they called her Ashpet.

Well, one day they were all fixin' to go to church-meetin'. They never let Ashpet go anywhere. They knew she was prettier than the old woman's two girls, and if anybody came to the house they always shoved Ashpet under a wash tub. That day, just when they were tryin' to get fixed up to go to meetin', their fire went out, so they had to borrow fire. Now there was an old witch-woman lived over the gap in the mountain. These rich folks, they wouldn't have nothin' to do with this old woman but they had to have fire so they sent the oldest one of the girls over there to borrow some fire. The oldest girl she went traipsin' on over the gap. She thought herself so good she didn't go in the house, just stuck her hand through a crack in the logs.

"I come after fire."

"Come in and comb my hair and I'll give ye some."

"I'll not put my pretty clean hands on your old cat-comb!"

"You'll get no fire."

The old woman she sent the next-oldest. She went a-swish-in' up the hill and through the gap. She was so nice! She ran her hand through that crack.

"I want some fire."

"Come in and comb my hair."

"Me? Put my nice white hands on your old cat-comb?"

"Put off then. You'll get no fire."

Then the old woman hollered for Ashpet. And Ashpet she went on up through the gap, ran down the holler, and went right on in the house.

"Good evenin', Auntie."

"Good evenin', Ashpet."

"'I want to borry a coal of fire, please, ma'm."

"Comb my hair and you can have it."

Ashpet combed her hair for her, and then the old woman gave her some fire: put it in an old dried toadstool.[3]

"You goin' to meetin', Ashpet?"

"Law, no! They never let me go anywhere at all. I got to wash the dishes and scour the pots. I'll not get done till meet-in's plumb over."

"You want to go?"

"Why, yes, I'd like that the best in the world!"

---

3. That's the way they used to carry fire: take an old hard-dried toadstool, the kind that grows kind of like a shelf on the side of a dead tree, cut it on the edge and put a hot coal there till it would start burning around inside. You could hold fire nearly a week that way.

"Time they all get good and gone, I'll be up there to see you."

Ashpet she ran on back over the mountain and built up the fires, got in wood and water, and went to milkin' and feedin'. She had to hurry 'cause she had supper to cook, too. Then they eat supper, and Ashpet helped the two girls get fixed up, and fin'lly they all went on off to meetin'. When they were all out of sight down the road here came that old witch-woman a-hobblin' through the gap with her stick. She walked in the house, went on out to the kitchen, says to Ashpet, says, "You just keep right still there by the door now."

So Ashpet looked in the kitchen door; and the old woman set all the dishes on one end of the table and the dishpan on the other end and hit full of scaldin' water. Then she knocked on the table, says:

> *"All dirty dishes stay off the shelf!*
> *Get in the water, shake yourself!*
> *Wash, dish! Wash!"*

And the plates and platters and cups and saucers and bowls and knives and forks and spoons ran over and slipped through the hot water and rose up and shook themselves and hopped up on the shelves just as clean and dry as anybody'd have to do in an hour's hard work. Then the old woman she opened the back door, says:

> *"Pots and skillets — handle and spout!*
> *Get in the sand and scour out!*
> *Scrub, pot! Scrub!"*

And it was a sight in the world how every pot and pan and kettle and skillet went hoppin' and straddlin' out the door and rolled down to the creek and went to rubbin' and scrapin' in the sand and dippin' in the water, and then they all came bumpin' back in the house and settled down by the hearth-rock right where they

belonged. Ashpet had an awful good time watchin' all that. She nearly laughed herself to death.

Then the old woman reached in her apron pocket, took out a mouse, and an old piece of leather and a rawhide string, two scraps of shoe-leather, and an old piece of rag. She put the mouse down before the door, laid that chunk of leather on it, dropped that rawhide string over its head, says:

> *"Co-up, little mare!*
> *Whoa now! Whoa!"*

— and there stood the finest little pied-ed mare you ever saw: pretty new saddle and bridle on it, and it was just as gentle as a girl 'uld want. Then that old witch-woman she knocked that piece of rag around this way and that, laid it on the bed; took the two scraps of leather, knocked them up a time or two, set 'em under the bed, says, "Now, Ashpet, you shut your eyes and wish for the dress and slippers you want to wear to meetin'."

Ashpet shut her eyes and wished and when she opened 'em there was a pretty red dress stretched out on the coverlet, and under the bed were the prettiest red slippers — the littlest 'uns you ever saw. Then Ashpet she washed herself and put on her red dress and slippers.

"Now," says the old woman, "quick as meetin' breaks, you get back here and hide your horse in the bresh, and hide your dress and slippers, and put on your old ashy clothes again."

Ashpet went ridin' on up to the church-house, and tied her horse and walked in the door. Everybody saw her, but nobody knew who she was. Now the King's son was there and he kept his eyes right on her. When meetin' started breakin' he followed Ashpet, and saw her get on her little mare and turn its head to go, so he jumped on his horse and took out after her. She paid no attention but he caught up with her directly, started talkin' to her.

They rode on a piece, and then she eased off one of her slippers and kicked it in the bresh; rode on a little piece farther, says, "I've lost one of my slippers, sure's the world! It must have dropped off in the road somewhere between here and the church-house."

"I'll get it for you," he told her. "You wait here now." And he turned his horse and went back. But time he was out of sight she galloped her little mare on in home, hid it in the woods, ran to the house and hid her dress and slipper, got her old ashy dress again and went to sweepin' and dustin'.

That boy had a time findin' her slipper but fin'lly he saw it there in the bresh, picked it up, and when he rode on back and found the girl gone he didn't know what in the world to do.

Well, he took that little red slipper and went all over the country lookin' for the one it would fit. Got down there where the old woman and the two girls lived at fin'lly; and when they saw him comin' they grabbed Ashpet and run with her and stuck her under that washtub.

The King's son came on in with the slipper, says, "This slipper came off the prettiest woman in the world, and the one it fits is the one I'll marry."

The oldest 'un she took the slipper and ran out behind the house; took a knife and trimmed her heel and her toes till she made it fit. The boy looked at her other foot and he got suspicious; and just about that time a little bird flew to the door and started singin':

> *"Trim your heels, and trim your toes!*
> *Under the tub the slipper goes!"*

"What did you say, little bird?"

"Shoo!" says the old woman, and the bird flew off.

The King's son he jerked the slipper off that girl and he saw how she'd trimmed her heel and her toes. So the next-oldest she grabbed up the slipper and ran out. She squeezed her foot in it, but she had to trim her heel and toes, too. Then that boy he looked at her foot and it was in the slipper all right but when he looked at her face he wasn't satisfied at all; so he pulled the slipper off again, and then he noticed where she had been trimmin' her heel and toes.

Then that little bird fluttered at the door again—

> *"Trim your heels, and trim your toes!*
> *Under the tub the slipper goes!"*

"SHOO!" hollered the old woman.

But the King's son he watched the bird and it flew out in the yard and lit on that tub—

> *"Trim your heels, and trim your toes!*
> *Under the tub the slipper goes!"*

So the boy went out and lifted the tub and looked in under it, and there was Ashpet.

"What you doin' under there?"

"They always put me under here."

"Come on out."

"I'm too ragged and dirty."

"You try this slipper on. Here!"

So Ashpet stuck out her foot and he put the slipper on it and it fitted perfect. Then she went and washed her face and put on her red dress and her other slipper; ran out in the bresh and got her horse, and she and the King's son rode on off and got married.

Well, the two girls and the old woman they acted awful nice after the weddin', went up to the King's house several times and they always brought Ashpet somethin'. Then one day the girls told her about a fine place to go swimmin', says, "Let's go up there today and go in. Come on and go with us, Ashpet."

So they took Ashpet up to the swimmin' place and both the girls acted like they were goin' in the water but they let Ashpet go in first. They knew that an Old Hairy Man lived in that hole of water; and when Ashpet went in, he got her. The two girls laughed and went on home.

The Old Hairy Man kept Ashpet in a cave in the bank over that deep water, and she couldn't get away from him. There wasn't any boat, and the water was swift and it licked right up to the mouth of the cave. Well, after Ashpet was there a day or so the Old Hairy Man got to braggin' about how his hide was so thick there couldn't no ball nor bullet hurt him.

"Can't hurt ye *nowhere?*" Ashpet asked him.

"Nowhere," he told her, " — except a little mole back of my left shoulder. If I was to get hit there it 'uld lay me out, cold."

Now the King's son had done raised an army to hunt for his wife, and they fin'lly came by that cave. Ashpet ran out and stood over that deep hole and they saw her.

"Shoot him in the back of his left shoulder!" she hollered to 'em. Then she ran and hid behind a big rock.

The men they got some boats and rowed across and shot in the mouth of the cave. Here came Old Hairy Man a-scrapin' and a-gruntin', and he went to grabbin' the men out the boats and throwin' 'em back across the river as fast as they landed, but they got more boats and landed on both sides of that cave. They kept on shootin' but the bullets and balls just glanced off the Old Hairy Man's hide, and he kept right on fightin' and a-throwin' the men every which-a-way. But fin'lly the King's boy and some of his men got in behind him and they went to aimin' back of his left shoulder until one ball happened to hit that mole — and that fixed him — knocked him out, cold.

So they took Ashpet and ran for life, rowed across in a hurry. Old Hairy Man he came to about the time they landed on the other side, and he went to jumpin' up and down a-hollerin', "You got my woman!"

Well, as soon as the King's boy got Ashpet home safe, he went and arrested that old woman and her two girls, carried 'em down to that deep hole of water and threw 'em in. Says, "Here's ye *three* women!"

And Old Hairy Man he came out and grabbed 'em and hauled 'em in his cave — and they're down there yet, I reckon.

A girl spoke out from somewhere in the back of the room, "I know one — about a King, and his daughters."

The child told the tale slowly, thinking ahead now and then before she spoke. I couldn't see her, and it was as though the tale came out of the night.

LIKE MEAT LOVES SALT

One time there was a very old King and he had three daughters. And one day he asked 'em what would they like for
him to buy 'em in town. The girls were plannin' on goin' to a dance
that night so the first one she told him she wanted a dark-flash-
ing green dress; the second one asked for a bright-flashing red
dress; and then the youngest (the King loved her better'n the others)
said that she wanted a dress that was solid white.

The old King got on his horse and went on to town and got the
three dresses, and on the way back a bough of maple hit his hat.
He reached up and broke it off; and when he looked at it, it was
full of white roses. Well, he came on in home and got back on his
throne and called his oldest girl. And when she came in he asked
her, says, "How much do you love me?"

"Oh," she says, "I love you more than life."

So he put a white rose on her green dress and gave it to her,
and she took it and went to get ready to go to the dance.

Then he called his next-oldest girl and asked her how much did she love him.

"Why," she says, "I love you more than I can tell ye."

So he put a white rose on her red dress and she took it and went on to get fixed up to go to that dance. Then he called his youngest girl and says, "Now you tell me — how much do you love your old daddy?"

She thought a minute then she told him, "I love you like meat loves salt."

"Is that your answer?" he asked her, real mad-like.

"Yes," she says, "I love you as much as my duty will let me, and that's the dyin' truth."

That made him even madder, so he hid her dress, and then he locked her up in a high tower on the prairies. Never let her see anybody, except one old woman to get her water and cook for her.

And she was sittin' in the window one day combin' her hair and lettin' the tears fall — and the Duke of England rode by and looked up there and saw her. A grapevine ran up the tower right to the window; so the Duke of England he climbed up that vine and carried that girl down; took her across the ocean and married her.

Well, the two other girls had got married and gone off with their husbands, and the old King got lonesome, so one day he went to live with his oldest daughter. She greeted him well, but he hadn't been there more'n a few days when she told him, says, "You'll have to do without your servants. There's not enough room here for 'em." And she sent 'em off — all but two. So then the old King went to stay with his next-oldest daughter, and she fired his last two servants and put him in the stable to sleep. Then he knew that his two oldest daughters didn't really love him, so he went on off by himself.

Then the two girls' husbands, they started raisin' war on the Duke of England, and fin'lly the Duke brought his army across the ocean; and they all started in fightin'. The youngest girl she had come with the Duke and they went out walkin' in the country one day, and they found the old King a-wanderin' around crazy. He'd done twisted himself a crown out of honeysuckle vines. And he didn't know his youngest girl when she came up to him. She and the Duke took him with 'em, and they went on across the country, and directly they saw the two oldest girls caught in a thornbush and just a-screamin'.

The youngest asked 'em, says, "What are you doin' in that thornbush?"

"Our husbands put us in here."

"Good enough for ye!" said the old King.

Well, the Duke he won the war, and then they took the old King with 'em across the water. And one day the girl told the cook not to put any salt in the meat. So when the King started eatin' his dinner he said the meat didn't taste right. His daughter brought him a dish of salt; didn't say a word, just stood there. Then the

old King knew her, and he got his mind back again; and then he sent a servant across the water to get that white dress where he'd hidden it, and when he gave it to his youngest daughter it had a bough of white roses on it—and the roses were just as fresh as if they'd been picked that very day.

The voice in the shadows ceased. For a moment there was no sound except the soft crackling and hissing of the fire. I had written rapidly, trying to record every word, and my arm ached—and my eyes had misted up a bit. Tom had stopped carving. He sat with his head erect as though listening at something far off. A stick burned in two and fell in the midst of the fire.

Sarah broke the silence. "I heard a funny one from Aunt Nell Adams the other day. Her girl was home from Cincinnati with her three boys, and you should have heard them kids laugh while Old Nell told 'em that tale."

"Well, Sary!" exclaimed Old Rob. "I never did hear you tell ar' tale yet."

"I don't know whether I can tell it right or not."

"Go on and tell it," commanded Granny.

SOAP, SOAP, SOAP!

One time there was a woman fixin' to wash clothes and she found out she didn't have no soap, so she hollered for her little boy and told him to go to the store for soap, says, "Don't you forget now — *soap*."

So he headed for the store, a-runnin' along and sayin', "Soap! soap! soap!" — so he wouldn't forget. Come to a slick place in the road and he slipped and fell. Got up again, went on, tried to think what it was his mommy sent him for and he couldn't remember. So he walked back to where he slipped, says, "Right there I had it."

Walked on a few steps, stopped, says, "Right there I lost it."

Walked back — "Right there I had it."

Walked on again — "Right there I lost it."

Kept on walkin' back and forth sayin', "Right there I had it — Right there I lost it" — till he had him a regular loblolly there in the road — had mud mired plumb over the tops of his shoes. Man come along directly and heard what he was sayin'. Asked him, says, "What ye lost?"

> *"Right there I had it —*
> *Right there I lost it."*

"What ye lost? I'll help ye find it."

> *"Right there I had it —*
> *Right there I lost it."*

So the man thought he was crazy and started on by, and he slipped in the boy's loblolly and like to fell. Says, "That blame mud! Hit's slick as soap."

"Soap! soap! soap!" says the boy and started on off again. And that man thought the boy was mockin' him so he stepped over and grabbed him and shook him, says, "You say you're sorry and won't do it again, or I'll whip you good."

"Sorry I done it; won't do it again—
Sorry I done it; won't do it again."

So the man turned him loose and the boy run on; but he started in sayin' that and couldn't think of the soap. Got down the road and come across an old woman had fell in the ditch and broke all the eggs she had in her basket. She was gettin' up about the time that boy come along—

"Sorry I done it; won't do it again—
Sorry I done it; won't do it again."

And the old woman thought he was makin' fun of her, so she grabbed him and boxed his ears, and then she pushed him in the ditch, says, "I'm out and you're in."

And when he got out the ditch he went on, sayin':

"I'm out and you're in.
I'm out and you're in."

Come to where a man had one wagon wheel mired 'way down in a mudhole and was tryin' to get it out—

"I'm out and you're in.
I'm out and you're in."

The man grabbed him, says, "You oughtn't say that. One's out and now you come here and help me get the other'n out—or I'll whup you good."

So the boy had to help him, and when they got it out on down the road he went—

"One's out; get the other'n out—
One's out; get the other'n out."

And a one-eyed man come along and that boy went past him —

"One's out; get the other'n out —
One's out; get the other'n out."

So the one-eyed man grabbed him and he just smoked that boy's britches. Says, "You oughtn't say sech a thing to me. You might 'a said 'One's in anyway!'" Turned him loose, and on the boy went —

"One's in anyway —
One's in anyway."

Come to where a woman was washin' clothes at her washin' place in the creek 'side the road. Her two least young 'uns was runnin' around there playin' and one of 'em had slipped and fell in the creek. The woman run to get it out and just about that time there was that boy —

"One's in anyway —
One's in anyway."

So she jerked the young 'un out the creek, and then she went after that boy and grabbed him, and she was about to give him a

good paddlin' for makin' fun of her and her young 'uns but when she saw how dirty he was where he'd been in the mud so many times and been cryin' and wipin' his face with his muddy hands, she took pity sake on him and turned him loose, says, "You run on back home and tell your mommy to take some soap and wash that black face."

Time he heard "Soap" he lit out down the road—

"Soap! Soap! Soap!—
Soap! Soap! Soap!"

And that time he got to the store and got the soap and run on home with it and handed it to his mommy. And she give him one look and then she took him by the ear and marched him down to her wash-place and soused him in the creek — clothes and all. Then she soaped him all over — with his britches and his shirt right on him. Soused him ag'in, till she got all the mud and dirt off him.

Then she took two clothespins and hung him up on her clothes-line by his shirt-tail, and left him there to dry while she got the rest of her washin' done.

Another father came for his kids while Sarah was in the midst of her story. He looked around, nodded to Tom and the rest of us, took a chair vacated for him by one of the boys — and stayed; and when the tale was done he asked, "You all keepin' Old-Christmas Eve?"

"We come over here with Tom every year on the night of the fifth," Old Rob answered him, "and you ought to have seen the old dumb-show these boys put on for us tonight. Old Kel's known it all his life, but this is the first time any of us ever saw it all acted out right."

"There was one speech they left out," said Uncle Kel. "That young 'un who played the Doctor's part just couldn't memorize it."

"I tried to," came a voice from the chimney corner. "It was too long. I'd 'a got all tangled up if I'd tried to put it in."

"What was it, Kel? Can you say it?" asked Tom.

Uncle Kel laughed. "Old Bet asks the Doctor how far he's ever traveled, and the Doctor says —"

THE
SKOONKIN HUNTIN'

T raveled this world all over: house to the barn, upstairs, down-
stairs, out the front door plumb to the gate — and then me
and Paw started gettin' fixed to go on that larrapin' rarrapin' tarrapin' skoonkin huntin'. So Paw went out to round up all the dogs,
all but Old Shorty. And I went and shucked and shelled the pigs
a bucket of slop, but when I got down there the punkins was all
in the pig-patch, so I picked up a pig and knocked them punkins
out of there. Took my bridle out to the chicken-house, slung it on
the barn, led the old stump up 'side the horse, throwed the saddle
across the fence, jumped a-straddle with both legs on one side,
rode down a long straight road that wound all around the mountains, came to a house made of cornbread shingled with flap-jacks,
knocked on the woman and a door came out, asked her for a crust
of beer and a glass of light-bread, told her no-thank-you-ma'am-
please-I-don't-care-for-some-I-just-had-any. Bark came along and
dogged at me, so I ran on till I came to a little valley town sittin'

'way up on a hill—little roast pigs runnin' up and down the streets with knives and forks stuck in their backs squealin' "Who'll eat me? Who'll eat me?"—Went on to my brother's place. Easy to find it—little brick house made out of logs standin' all by itself in the middle of forty-four others just like it. My old mare stumbled and throwed me over her head and tail right face foremost flat on my back and tore my hide and bruised my shirt; so I went on down to see my gal Sal. She was awful glad to see me—had both doors nailed down and both windows nailed up, so I went on in and throwed my hat on the fire and stirred up the bed and we sat down right close together, she in one corner and me in the other and talked about love and politics and dog-ticks and bed-ticks and straw-ticks and beggar-ticks and we played cards and she drawed a heart and I drawed a diamond and about that time her old man came home and he drawed a club and I says, "Good-bye, honey, and if I never see ye no more the old gray mare is yours." So Paw he had all the dogs rounded up by then — all but Old Shorty, and then he rounded him up too; and the dogs all trailed — all but Old Shorty, and then he trailed too; and directly they all treed — all but Old Shorty, then he treed too; so I cloomb up that siceyebucky-more tree 'way out on a chestnut limb sittin' on a pine knot and I shook and I shook, and directly somethin' hit the ground and I looked around — and it was me; and every blame one of them dogs jumped on me — all but Old Shorty, then he jumped too; so I knocked 'em all off — all but Old Shorty and I grabbed him by the tail and cut his tail off right up close behind his ears. So we got back in home from that larrapin', rarrapin', tarrapin', skoonkin huntin', had two 'possum tails, two black eyes, four skinned-up shank bones, no horse, and all the dogs — all but Old Shorty.

This kept the boys doubled over with laughter. Then Tom spoke out, "Another'n just came to my mind. Hit's a tale my wife used to tell our kids 'fore they growed up; and now their children ask for it every time they come from Roanoke to see me. The way my wife told it — "

PRESENTNEED, BYMEBY, AND HEREAFTER

One time there was an old man and he never had married; and he got tired of tryin' to keep house by himself, so he went and found him an old woman and married her and took her on home. It was about hog-killin' time then, and that old woman she didn't like to work a bit, but she went on out to watch the old man put up the meat in the smokehouse. He was a-sortin' it out, says, "Now these backbones and ribs, that's for present need and we'll lay it here; and we'll hang the shoulders and hams over here, and that's for by and by; and we'll put all this sowbelly and fatback up there, and that'll be for hereafter."

Then he looked down at the big tub of lard he had, all rendered out, says, "And look at all that lard! Won't that be fine to grease cabbage heads with!" He just loved fried cabbage.

The old woman she listened to every word, kept noddin' her head —and directly they got the hog-meat all put away for the winter.

Well, one day pretty soon after that the old man left to go off on a trip somewhere, and the next day a man rode up in the yard, and hollered hello. The old woman came to the door.

"What can I do for ye?"

"Is the man of the house here?"

"No, he left yesterday. Said he'd be gone all week."

"Well, I had a little business with him. I'll have to come back next week, I reckon."

"What's your name?"

"Presnell Sneed."

"O Mister Presentneed! I know exactly what ye come for: you want your meat. He's got a *pile* of meat here for ye. I'm glad you've done come to get it; hit'll be out the way."

Well, that feller was sort of surprised; but he saw it was a chance to get him a little meat, so he said all right, bein' as he was there he'd take the meat on with him.

"But I forgot to bring me a sack," he told her.

"Aw, that's all right; we got plenty of sacks here."

The old lady went and hunted him up some tow-sacks and took 'em on out to the smokehouse, and she helped that man to get all them backbones and ribs packed and helped him get 'em loaded on behind the saddle. And just when he was about to start off she hollered out to him, says, "O Mister Presentneed! He's got some meat here for Mister Bymeby too. If you was to meet him anywhere down the road you tell him he can come on and get his meat, jest any time. Tell him to bring some sacks. We ain't got no more."

He told her he sure would; and then he rode down the road a piece and dumped the meat out them sacks; swapped hats with a man in the road, and directly he pulled on back to the old man's house.

"Hello! Hello! Is there anybody home?"

She looked out the door. "What can I do for ye?"

"Howdy do, ma'm. My name's Bymeby, and I want to see your man on a little business."

"Well, your meat's a-hangin' out there in the smokehouse. That's what ye come for, I reckon. Jest get down and come on in. I'll go out there with ye and show ye which meat's your'n."

She helped him get them hams and shoulders all sacked up and loaded on his horse; says, "Now we got meat here for Mister Hereafter, too. If you run across him down the road anywhere would ye mind tellin' him he can come on here for his meat? — jest any time. You tell him to be sure and bring some sacks."

"All right, ma'm. If I see him I'll be sure to tell him."

So that feller he went and dumped them sacks again. Then he turned his coat inside out and in a few minutes there he was back at the old man's front gate a-hollerin' hello.

"Howdy do, stranger."

"Howdy do, ma'm. I come to see your man on business. My name's Hereafter."

"Jest get down and come on in, Mister Hereafter. I see you brought some sacks to pack your meat in. Hit's out yonder in the smokehouse: that big pile of middlin's. You can go on out there and get it. I'd help ye but I been helpin' them men pack meat all mornin' and I'm plumb give out. Now that meat business is out the way, and I'm glad of it."

Well, that feller he had to hire him a wagon to haul all his meat off. He took it on to town and sold it; made him a pile of money.

The old woman got rested up after a while, and then she remembered that lard, so she thought she'd finish the job right for her old man. She went and dragged the lard tub clean on out in the field where the cabbage patch was at, and up one row and down the next — a-greasin' all the cabbage heads with the old man's lard. And just when she got the last head covered with the last smear of grease in the tub, she looked behind her and there was the old hound-dog had follered her every step a-lickin' off the lard just as hard as it could lick.

And when the old man got in home that Saturday night she stepped out to meet him — "Well, old man, you've done had the best luck! All them men come and got their meat."

The old man's eyes popped open. "What men?"

"Why, Mister Presentneed and Mister Bymeby, and Mister Here-after — the ones you said the meat was for."

The old man ran and looked in the smokehouse; came back just a-r'arin', says, "And what in the nation have ye done with all my lard?"

"Why, I done what you said: I greased the cabbage heads with it."

"All of it?"

"Why sure."

"Have you done gone and cut that whole field of cabbage heads, old woman?"

"Law, no!" she says. "You never said cut 'em; I jest greased 'em right where they was at. But that old no-'count hound of your'n come along and licked it ever' bit off."

"You're plumb crazy, old woman! And I'm goin' to leave you, that's what I'm a-goin' to do. I'll not live with ye another minute."

And out the gate he put. She hollered after him, says, "Well, if you leave, I'm a-goin' to leave, too."

He hollered back at her, says, "Don't you leave the house with-out you wrop up the fire, and be sure you pull the door after ye."

He meant for her to cover the fire with ashes so the house wouldn't be liable to burn down, and to shut the door behind her. Well — that old woman she ran to the fireplace and wropped her apron full of hot coals and ashes; held 'em up with one hand, and then she wrenched the door off its old rickety hinges and pulled it after her down the path and on out the front gate.

And when the old man heard that door-shutter a-bangin' on the rocks in the road he looked back, and there came his old woman in a light-flame! The smoke was just a-pourin' and the door a-jumpin' up and down behind her. So he ran back and put her out, turned around and started walkin' on off again — right on down the road, never looked back or nothin'. And the old woman she took off right in after him, with a big hole burnt in her apron, and her face all sooted up, and that door a-knockin' and a-bangin' all over the road.

They went on and went on, and the old man he tried to out-walk her but she pulled right on in behind him. And fin'lly he gained on her a little; then he saw a big sycamore 'side the road, so he thought he'd see could he get shet of her; ran over to that tree and went to climbin' it. But she saw him, and the next thing he knowed here she come right on up in the tree a-pullin' the door up with her. He cloomb plumb to the top and sat down in a fork; and she got out on a limb right beside him and there she sat a-holdin' on to that door. Neither one of 'em spoke a word.

Well, directly here came a gang of robbers down the road and they walked over there under that tree and sat down to divide out the money they'd stole that day. The old man was scared to death they'd look up there and shoot him down, but they kept watchin' about the money they were pullin' out their pockets. And just about the time the robbers got all their money in a big pile the old woman says, "Old man, I can't hold on to this door much longer."

He whispered to her, says, "O law, old woman! Don't you let go that thing! They'll shoot us down out of here, both of us!"

"Why, I'm bound to drop it!"

"Hush! Don't talk so loud! If you drop that door, old woman, I'll kick ye out of here, sure's the world."

"Well, I can't help that," says the old woman; and her holt slipped —

A-WHAMMITY BANG!
BANG! CLATTERY BANG!
WHAM-BANG!

— down through the tree that door rattled; and time she let go her holt the old man hauled his foot back and let her have it. The old woman she tumbled down out of there, and the door it would

get caught on the limbs and then she'd light on top of it; then it 'uld turn over with her and they'd fall again, but somehow or other every time the door caught she'd light on in, and when the door hit the ground there was the old woman a-sittin' right on it! Her clothes was sort of mussed up but she wasn't even scratched.

Well, them robbers had pulled out and they were a mile away from there time the door and the old woman hit the ground. When they heard all that racket up above they thought it was the end of time — and they'd run for life!

They quit runnin' after they were good and gone: slowed up and started talkin' about it. They took notice that the rest of the sky wasn't fallin' and they got to wonderin'; so fin'lly they stopped and sent one rogue back to find out what'n-all had happened.

So one of 'em went on back and slipped around, slipped around and looked out from behind some bushes — and there was the old woman a-standin' guard over all that money and a-gatherin' it up in her skirts; the old man he was just hangin' around.

Well, that robber he didn't know whether she was a witch or what, with her apron burnt off and her face all blacked up and her hair all scorched out every which-a-way; but he came on out the bresh sort of scared-like, and eased on over there closer to her until fin'lly he was up fairly near the tree. Then the old woman she went to singin'. The rogue he tried to think of somethin' to say, so directly he told her, says, "You sure can sing good."

"Yes," she says, "I always did like to sing. Can you sing?"

"No, I never was any good at singin'."

"Did ye ever have your tongue clipped?"

"No, don't know as I ever did."

"Why, that's what's the matter you can't sing! Stick your tongue out here."

The old woman looked at his tongue right hard, says, "Law me! No wonder you can't sing! Hold right still now and I'll clip your tongue for ye: won't charge you a cent."

So she tucked her skirts in her belt so's not to drop her money; and then she ran her hand in her blouse-front where she'd laid a couple of clothespins that mornin', that kind — you know — that have got a little steel spring in 'em.

"Stick out your tongue. Jest a little farther now."

And she clipped them clothespins on the man's tongue. He couldn't see down on his face there and he thought sure's the world she'd done clipped his tongue off. He broke and run — tore up the bushes gettin' away from there!

The other robbers saw him comin', hollered at him, says,

"What was it?"

"What made all that racket?"

"Did ye get our money?"

"Thaw thaw thawm! Thaw thong-n-n, thaw!" was all he could say.

And they thought he'd done got witched and was runnin' crazy, so all the robbers jumped up from there and down the road they flew! They ran plumb over the boundary and never was seen again.

The old woman she finished gatherin' up that money — the old man he had snitched him a few dollars while she wasn't lookin' — and she started on back home holdin' it in her skirt and hit just a-jinglin'. And she never had to do a lick of work from then on.

And the old man he tagged right on in home behind her; he decided he'd not leave her after all — not right then, anyhow.

"Law!" said Granny. "That's like Sam and Sooky, and I've not thought of that 'un for over forty years. Wait till I light my pipe."

Kel handed her his twist and knife. She sliced off a bit of tobacco, rubbed it in her palm, and let it run in her little reed-stemmed clay pipe. Stan had a lit splinter ready for her. She puffed slowly a time or two, and then leaned over, pipe in hand.

"I reckon it'll all come to me — "

SAM AND SOOKY

Well . . . Sam and Sooky they got married and started in housekeepin'.

"I'm goin' to farm, Sooky. What you goin' to do for your occupation?"

"Why, I don't know."

"How are ye about cardin' wool?"

"Oh, I can card. Allus did see 'em card when I was back home with my mammy."

So Sammy went and worked on the public roads till he got him enough money to buy Sooky a pair of wool-cards, brought 'em on home. And next day Sammy went to clearin' for a little garden patch, and Sooky she got holt of an old fleece and sat down and went to cardin'. The cards — you know — they always make a sort of scrapin' fuss, and Sooky heard 'em sayin' —

Lazy! Lazy! Lazy!

"I ain't no sech a thing!"

Lazy! Lazy! Lazy!

"You hush now! If you say that again I'll throw ye in the fire."

Lazy! Lazy! Lazy!

Sooky threw the cards in the fire, and went to sweepin' and dustin' and housekeepin'.

Sammy came in that evenin'. "How much cardin' did ye get done?"

"Ain't done none!"

"How come?"

"I throwed the con-founded things in the fire!"

"You did? Why in the nation did ye do that?"

"I went to cardin' and your blame' old cards kept callin' me *Lazy! Lazy!* I told 'em to hush and they just kept right on, so I burnt 'em up."

"Law me! You'll have to get ye some other occupation. How are ye about spinnin'?"

"Oh, I can spin. Allus did see 'em spin when I was back home. My mammy, she all the time spun."

So they eat supper — cornbread and water — and went on to bed.

Sammy went on back to workin' on the roads next day; worked till he got enough money for to buy Sooky a big spinnin' wheel; took him a few days that time. Toted the big wheel on home to Sooky. And the next day he went on with his clearin'. And Sooky she pulled the wheel out in front of the fire and went to spinnin'. The old wheel started whirrin'.

Widder-r-r! Widder-r-r! Widder-r-r!

"I ain't no widow-woman neither!"

Widder-r-r! Widder-r-r! Widder-r-r-r-r!

"You hush! I ain't no sech a thing! I got me a man; he's out yonder a-workin' in the bresh!"

WIDDer-r-r! WID-D-D-der-r-r-r! Widder-r-r!

"I'll fix ye, ye hateful thing — callin' me a widder!" Sooky got the axe and busted that wheel into kindlin' wood; laid it on the fire.

Sam came home. "Where's your wheel at?"

"Hit's there in the fire."

"O law, Sooky! What ye done now?"

"I ain't goin' to take nothin' off no old spinnin' wheel and hit callin' me a widder like it done. I burnt it up for tellin' lies on me that-a-way."

Well, Sam told Sooky not to bother no more about any occupation. So they eat their cornbread and had water to drink and went on to bed.

Next mornin' he says to her, says, "Sooky, I'm gettin' tired of nothin' but cornbread to eat. How are ye about biscuits?"

"Oh, I can cook biscuits. My mammy she cooked the best biscuits you ever tasted. I allus seen 'em cook when I was back at home."

Sam he went back on the county roads again till he'd worked out a twenty-four-pound poke of flour; took it on in home. Next mornin' he went on a-grubbin' and pilin' bresh in his garden patch.

Sooky she took and dumped that whole twenty-four pounds of flour out on the kitchen table, but 'fore she turned around to get her lard and water and start mixin', a gnat was buzzin' at her nose; and when she went to swat at it she knocked it in the flour. So she tried to get it out; looked for it, and looked for it, but she couldn't find it. And fin'lly she gathered up the corners of the oilcloth and took her flour on out in the yard; and then she started fannin' the flour to look for that gnat. She fanned it and fanned it till she fanned it every bit out in the grass. Never did find that gnat.

Sam came in; nothin' but two little corncakes sittin' there on the table. "Where's my light-bread biscuits, Sooky?"

"Do you want to eat biscuits with gnats in the dough?"

"Why, no."

"Well, a gnat got in my flour and I tried and I tried to get the blame thing out, but the flour was all gone 'fore I could find it." And she told him where the flour was at. So they eat their cornbread and water and went on to bed.

Next mornin' he says to her, says, "Sooky, I'm gettin' tired of just water to drink. How are ye about cookin' coffee?"

"Oh, I can cook coffee. My mammy she allus did make the best coffee — when I stayed back home."

So Sammy he worked out ten pounds of coffee, and brought it on home. — That was back in old times when they didn't have nothin' but green coffee beans: had to parch it and grind it at home. — So Sam handed the poke to Sooky, told her to have some good coffee for his supper that night; and he went on out to clear some more bresh.

Sooky she set the big pot on the fire, and when the water went to b'ilin' she dumped that ten pounds of green coffee beans in it and put in a big chunk of fat-meat.

Sam came in about dark. Cornbread and water on the table.

"Where's my coffee, Sooky?"

"That coffee you got, hit ain't no 'count. I been b'ilin' on it since twelve o'clock and hit's as raw now as when I put it in the pot."

Sammy went and looked in the pot, and there was his ten pounds of coffee — ruint.

Well, next mornin' Sam never said nothin' at all to Sooky. Went on out and went to clearin' his little patch of new ground. And about three o'clock Sooky went out to pick some blackberries. She didn't have her skirt pinned up very good, and after she'd got about a mile from the house the briars jerked her skirt off. She was pickin' so hard off'n a big heavy-loaded blackberry patch she never noticed her skirt was gone; went on pickin', pickin', picked on around to the other side of the patch; and then she scraped her knee against some briars — and she felt, and then she looked, and she didn't have a sign of a skirt on.

"O law!" she says. "Do you reckon this is me?"

She went on back and hid in the bresh close to where Sam was clearin', hollered, "Sammy!"

"What?"

"Where's Sooky at?"

"Why, she's at the house, I reckon."

Sooky says to herself, says, "Well! If Sooky's at the house and here I am out in the bresh — then it ain't me. I wonder who it is!"

And right about then I left from down there. So I don't know whether Sooky ever did find out who it was or not.

There were now five of the "least young 'uns" asleep on Tom's bed. A couple of boys in the chimney corner stretched and gaped, got up for another drink of water, and then settled themselves near Tom to watch him at his carving. The block of wood seemed to be shaping into a little man with his legs apart and fists clenched over his breast as though holding something.

"Well," called out Old Rob, "we done had about enough throwin' off on the womenfolks; here's a tale that's the other way around."

THE TWO
OLD WOMEN'S BET

One time there were two old women got to talkin' about the men folks: how foolish they could act, and what was the craziest fool thing their husbands had ever done. And they got to arguin', so fin'lly they made a bet which one could make the biggest fool of her husband.

So one of 'em said to her man when he come in from work that evenin', says, "Old man, do you feel all right?"

"Yes," he says, "I feel fine."

"Well," she told him, "you sure do look awful puny."

Next mornin' she woke him up, says, "Stick out your tongue, old man." He stuck his tongue out, and she looked at it hard, says, "Law me! You better stay in the bed today. You must be real sick from the look of your tongue."

Went and reached up on the fireboard, got down all the bottles of medicine and tonic was there and dosed the old man out of every bottle. Made him stay in the bed several days and she kept on talkin' to him about how sick he must be. Dosed him every few minutes and wouldn't feed him nothin' but mush.

Came in one mornin', sat down by the bed, and looked at him real pitiful, started in snifflin' and wipin' her eyes on her apron, says, "Well, honey, I'll sure miss ye when you're gone." Sniffed some more, says, "I done had your coffin made."

And in a few days she had 'em bring the coffin right on in beside the old man's bed. Talked at the old man till she had him thinkin' he was sure 'nough dead. And fin'lly they laid him out, and got everything fixed for the buryin'.

Well, the day that old woman had started a-talkin' her old man into his coffin, the other'n she had gone on to her house and about the time her old man came in from work she had got out her spinnin' wheel and went to whirlin' it. There wasn't a scrap of wool on the spindle, and the old man he fin'lly looked over there and took notice of her, says, "What in the world are ye doin', old woman?"

"Spinnin'," she told him, and 'fore he could say anything she says, "Yes, the finest thread I ever spun. Hit's wool from virgin sheep, and they tell me anybody that's been tellin' his wife any lies can't see the thread."

So the old man he come on over there and looked at the spindle, says, "Yes, indeed, hit surely is mighty fine thread."

Well, the old woman she'd be there at her wheel every time her old man come in from the field — spin and wind, spin and wind, and every now and then take the shuck off the spindle like it was full of thread and lay it in a box. Then one day the old man come in and she was foolin' with her loom, says, "Got it all warped off today. Just got done threadin' it on the loom." And directly she sot down and started in weavin' — step on the treadles, throwin' the shuttle and hit empty. The old man he'd come and look and tell her what fine cloth it was, and the old woman she 'uld weave right on. Made him think she was workin' day and night. Then one evenin' she took hold on the beam and made the old man help her unwind the cloth.

"Lay it on the table, old man — Look out! You're a-lettin' it drag the floor."

Then she took her scissors and went to cuttin'.

"What you makin', old woman?"

"Makin' you the finest suit of clothes you ever had."

Got out a needle directly and sat down like she was sewin'. And there she was, every time the old man got back to the house, workin' that needle back and forth. So he come in one evenin' and she says to him, "Try on the britches, old man. Here." The old man he shucked off his overalls and made like he was puttin' on the new britches.

"Here's your new shirt," she told him, and he pulled off his old one and did his arms this-a-way and that-a-way gettin' into his fine new shirt. "Button it up, old man." And he put his fingers up to his throat and fiddled 'em right on down.

"Now," she says, "Let's see does the coat fit ye." And she come at him with her hands up like she was holdin' out his coat for him, so he backed up to her and stuck his arms in his fine new coat.

"Stand off there now, and let me see is it all right. — Yes, it's just fine. You sure do look good."

And the old man stood there with nothin' on but his shoes and his hat and his long underwear.

Well, about that time the other old man's funeral was appointed and everybody in the settle-ment started for the buryin' ground. The grave was all dug and the preacher was there, and here came the coffin in a wagon, and fin'lly the crowd started gatherin'. And pretty soon that old man with the fine new suit of clothes came in sight. Well, everybody's eyes popped open, and they didn't know whether they ought to laugh or not but the kids went to gigglin' and about the time that old man got fairly close one feller laughed right out, and then they all throwed their heads back and laughed

good. And the old man he 'uld try to tell somebody about his fine new suit of clothes, and then the preacher busted out laughin' and slappin' his knee — and everybody got to laughin' and hollerin' so hard the dead man sat up to see what was goin' on. Some of 'em broke and ran when the corpse rose up like that, but they saw him start in laughin' — laughed so hard he nearly fell out the coffin — so they all came back to find out what-'n-all was goin' on.

The two old women had started in quarrelin' about which one had won the bet, and the man in the coffin heard 'em; and when he could stop laughin' long enough he told 'em, says, "Don't lay it on me, ladies! He's got me beat a mile!"

Tom's clock, hardly noticed until now, suddenly bonged eleven. Talk ceased for a minute or so. The two men who had come to take their children home still showed no signs of leaving. Steve moved to mend up the fire. The green backlog was glowing bright where it was beginning to char, and now the flames rose slowly as Steve fed them.

There was a general re-shifting of all the crowd, a bit more going in and out, the splash of the dipper in the red-cedar bucket, boys stretching and slumping again against each other. Jeems and two boys had gone out the door.

"Snow a-comin'!" Jeems proclaimed as he came back in. "I can smell it!"

Two little boys crawled up on the bed and promptly went off to sleep. The room settled into quietness again. Granny knocked her cold pipe against the hearth at her feet.

"There's a tale you've told us, Granny," said Delia, "that 'un about the two lost children. I'd like to hear it again."

Granny turned her head and glanced around at all of us: the sleeping children, the two big girls in straight chairs at the foot of the bed, the gang of boys sprawled near the fireplace and at each chimney corner, the circle of grown-ups, Tom whittling away, Jeems smoking, me with my chair tipped back against the oak chest, the lamp on Tom's dresser shining down on my big yellow pad.

"You been writin' down all them tales?"

"Just a scratch or two now and then to help me remember."

"Don't your hand give out writin' so much?"

"Yes'm, it does cramp a little sometimes."

"What tale was it you wanted, Deely?"

"Buck and Bess — and that other boy, Cooklepea."

Tom's big black cat had come in, and Granny reached down and stroked it. The cat purred loudly, arched its back against Granny's skirts, and squinted up at her. Granny kept fondling the big cat as she began her tale.

THE TWO LOST BABES

One time there was a man and a woman come from England to the U-nited States — back when this country was first settlin' up and families was scattered about in the wilderness. This man and his wife they had two children named Buck and Bess, and they lived 'way back in the mountains where it was solid woods. They had one little patch cleared for corn and beans but they had to live mostly off of wild game, and game had got so scarce they was about to starve. And one night the old woman started in talkin' to the old man, told him she didn't see how they could make out having two children to feed, said he ought to take 'em off and lose 'em in the wilderness — let 'em make out the best they could. So they decided to take Buck and Bess off the next day and leave 'em somewhere in the woods. Buck he had stayed awake and heard every word they said, so he slipped out just about daylight and picked up little white flint rocks till his pockets was full. Well, that mornin' the man took Buck and Bess 'way off in the wilderness and when they got a right long ways off from the house they come to a chestnut grove and he told the children to stay there and pick up chestnuts while he hunted some game. Left 'em there and put out. But Buck he told Bess, says, "Come on. No use in us waitin'." Buck he had dropped them rocks on the way. So he commenced followin' his trail of white flints and he and Bess got back in home about dark. The man told 'em, says, "Why, we was jest fixin' to start to hunt for ye. You must 'a not stayed where I told you to. We thought you was lost."

So the next mornin' he got up real early and took the children off 'fore daylight. So Buck didn't have no time to pick up rocks but he pulled a couple of ears of corn and hid 'em under his shirt-tail, and he 'uld shell off some grains every few steps. That time they went about twice as far, and then the old man left 'em and pulled out. Buck he tried to follow that trail of corn and he found it pretty well for about a half a mile but the squirrels and coons and 'possums and birds had come along and eat the corn. So that time the children really was lost. They tried to beat their way back but it got plumb thick dark. Bess she got awful scared 'cause they could hear the wolves howlin' and pan'ters screamin'. And then she give plumb out and Buck took her up on his back — told her not to cry, said he'd get her out all right.

Come to a big high rock-cliff after a while, cloomb up on it and saw a light off across the holler. Headed for where that light was at, come to a road and directly they found the house. Knocked on the door and an ugly-lookin' woman opened it. She told 'em to come on in. There was a boy there about Buck's size, named Cookle-pea. So the old woman give the three children some mush and milk and sent 'em up in the loft. Bess she went on off to sleep, but Buck and Cooklepea they got to talkin' and Cooklepea told Buck the old woman was a witch. Said she killed all the travelers that came by there and the only reason she hadn't killed him was she had to have somebody to cut her firewood. Said he never could get

away 'cause she had clip-boots that went a mile at a clip. So Cooklepea and Buck they made 'em a plan to try to get away. They slipped
shingles out the roof till they had a hole big enough to get out of,
and then they laid back down and made like they was sleepin'.

The old woman she got out a big butcher knife and commenced
whettin' it on her whet-rock. She whetted it a while, then she called
Cooklepea, "Cooklepea, you all asleep yet?"

"No'm."

So she went on whettin' her knife — *scrape, scrape, scrape.*

Then Buck and Cooklepea tied the corner of one of them quilts
to a rafter and put it out the hole and woke Bess up and helped
her out that hole and down to the ground.

Scrape, scrape, scrape.

"Cooklepea, you all asleep yet?"

"Bess is, but Buck and me ain't."

Scrape, scrape, scrape.

Then Buck and Cooklepea fixed the straw and the quilts so it
looked like Buck and Bess was still there a-sleepin', and then Cooklepea helped Buck out and down to the ground.

Scrape, scrape, scrape.

"Cooklepea, you all asleep yet?"

"Bess is, and Buck is, but I ain't."

Scrape, scrape, scrape.

Then Cooklepea he untied that quilt and fixed it so it looked
like he was under it, and then he crawled out the hole and Buck
and Bess helped him ease down to the ground. Then the three
children they slipped off from there and when they got out in the
road they run for life.

Scrape, scrape, scrape.

"Cooklepea, you all asleep yet?"

Scrape, scrape, scrape.

And when there didn't nobody answer, the old woman cloomb
up in the loft and slashed her old butcher-knife into Buck's and

Bess's quilts. Went on back down the ladder and went to sleep. And next mornin' she built her up a big fire to cook the two children. Hollered for Cooklepea to get up and cut some more wood, and when he never answered she went up in the loft and jerked up Cooklepea's quilt. Then she jerked up them other two quilts, and she was mad as time! Back down the ladder she went, and grabbed up her clip-boots, and out the door. She smelled around and smelled around till she smelled which-a-way the three children had gone, then she jerked on her clip-boots.

Well, Buck and Bess and Cooklepea they was sharp. They run to that big old rock-cliff and Cooklepea showed 'em where there was a long cave-like place back up under that rock — just was big enough for them to crawl in, and couldn't no grown person get in at all. So they slipped in there and went 'way back, and waited, and listened.

And time the old woman had her clip-boots on she took one step and there she was on top of that rock-cliff. Then she took off her clip-boots and smelled around up there till she traced them kids to the mouth of that little cave, and she tried to get in but she couldn't. So she reached in her long old skinny arm but she couldn't reach 'em either.

"O yes," she says, "I'll jest wait for ye. You'll git hongry enough in a few days."

So she went and laid down on top of that rock-cliff. Put her boots under her head and waited. She waited and waited, waited till about twelve but there wasn't a sound from them children, and the sun got good and warm and pretty soon the old woman went on off to sleep.

And when Buck and Bess and Cooklepea heard her snorin' they slipped up to the top of the rock-cliff, and Buck and Cooklepea give the old woman a quick shove and Bess she grabbed hold on them clip-boots. The old woman went rollin' and squallin' down that rock-cliff and landed in a briar thicket, and Bess handed Cooklepea the clip-boots right quick and when he got 'em on he grabbed Buck and Bess around the waist and lifted 'em up off the ground.

The old woman she'd done scrambled out the bresh and here she come a-tearin' back up the rock-cliff all scratched up and her hair full of leaves and trash, and she reached and made a grab for them children but 'fore she got there Cooklepea he took one step — and that put 'em a mile away from her.

So Cooklepea he held on to Buck and Bess and in about three more clips they landed in the lowland settle-ment. Then Cookle-pea took the boots off and they went to the sheriff and told him all about that old woman killin' folks.

"You may be right," he told 'em, "but you got to have evidence. You got any evi-dence?"

Cooklepea told him anyhow he could prove the old woman was a witch; said he knew when she had her witch meetin's. Said she was the head of a big gang of witches. So he told when the next witch meetin' was appointed, and they waited till that night. Then Cooklepea lent the sheriff the clip-boots and he took Cooklepea up on his back and Cooklepea showed him which way to head with them clip-boots. He stepped out and in just a few clips there they was at the old woman's house. So they looked through a crack in the logs and listened to the witches. After a while they heard one of 'em say, says, "Well, I've heard it told a woman never could keep a secret."

"That ain't so," says this old lady, "I've kept a secret. I been killin' travelers that come through here; melted lead and poured it in their ears while they was asleep, and robbed 'em and cooked 'em and eat 'em and buried the bones. Yes, indeed; and that's a secret I've kept more 'n thirty years."

Well, the sheriff went and banged on the door and hollered.

And all kinds of black cats jumped out the door time he opened it. And when they went in the house there wasn't a soul in there — just one old black cat. Hit come sidlin' up to 'em right friendly-

like but the sheriff he kicked it away and then it made for the door but Cooklepea already had the door shut. So then the sheriff hollered again and grabbed the black cat and shook it—and there was the old woman.

The sheriff arrested her and clipped on back to the settlement with her under one arm and Cooklepea under the other. And Buck and Bess and Cooklepea witnessed against the old woman and the sheriff he testified, too; and that was evi-dence enough so they burnt that old witch the next day.

And Cooklepea and Bess got married, and him and Buck went to clearin' land, and Bess she kept house for both of 'em. And Bess and Cooklepea had twelve young 'uns and they all done well.

Midnight

As Granny finished, the clock on the fireboard "scratched for midnight"—the short whirring sound that some old clocks make two or three minutes before the hour. Steve jumped up. "Let's go see the cows—whether they're praying or not!" And the whole gang of boys headed out the door.

"What's this," I asked when they were gone, "about the cows?"

"Don't you know?" Jeems answered me. "The cattle kneel down right on the stroke of midnight tonight."

"That's just a lot of old superstition," said Sarah.

"I've seen it," avowed Old Kel. "Me and some boys came in home late one Old-Christmas Eve, came in through the barn, and all the cows were standin' up and actin' restless-like, bothered; and then they commenced goin' down on their knees and one of 'em bawled right low and just horned the ground. Then they all laid down and was quiet and natural again. And we looked at the clock when we got to the house and it was about five minutes after twelve."

"I don't believe a word of it," snapped Sarah.

The clock struck midnight. Two of the small children turned over and mumbled in their sleep. We sat quite hushed for a few minutes. A far-away rooster crowed, another answered from Tom's back yard, and a third took up the cry from somewhere across the road. Tom stretched himself, got up and took the broom; swept his chips and whittlings into the fire, gave the whole hearth a brushing-up, and sat down again with his carving. The boys returned and sought their places without a word.

"Well, boys?" queried Old Kel.

"They never done nothin'," said Steve; "just laid there chewin' their cuds."

"That old clock of mine always did run about ten minutes a day slow," said Tom. "You must 'a just missed it, boys."

"Don't you know it's bad luck to watch for Old-Christmas signs a-purpose?" said Granny. "If you just happen to see ar' sign it's all right; but if you try to watch you'll be like the old man with the water-bucket."

"What was that, Granny?" asked Stan.

"Somebody told him water would turn to wine on Old-Christmas Eve; so he got the water-bucket full a few minutes before midnight and set it before him. He watched, and when the clock began to strike he hollered to his wife:

'Hit's turnin' to wine!'

and right then somethin' behind him says:

'Yes, and you're mine!'

And when the old woman came to look, the old man was gone, and they never knew what it was got him."

"Is it snowin' outside yet?" asked Jeems.

"No," said Steve, "but it's mighty still and dark, and cold."

Tom rose and laid knife and carving on the fireboard, and went out toward the back. Delia took the lamp and busied herself in the kitchen. Little Rob and Harry rolled themselves cigarettes. I made a trip to the water-bucket and stretched a bit. A boy crept over near the big girls and made some sort of teasing crack at them. Rhody swatted at him, he swatted back. She grabbed his hair and a merry scuffle took place. "You 'uns behave," warned Granny, and the boy shot back to his place in the chimney corner.

Tom came in carrying a big wooden bowl. "Here, Steve, you hand these apples around. You boys wait now till your turn. You can go out there and fill your pockets 'fore you leave."

Delia returned with the lamp in one hand and a large coffeepot in the other. Tom set the lamp back on the dresser and Delia and Steve soon had the coffeepot in place on the trivet. We all crunched apples — crisp, cool Winesaps they were.

"Onriddle this, boys," spoke up Old Rob. "If ye know it already don't tell.

> 'There was a man who had no eyes
> and he went out to view the skies;
> he saw a tree that had good apples grown,
> he took no apples off, he left no apples on.'

How was that now?"

"Don't make sense," droned one of the boys.

"Makes good sense if ye know it," Steve answered up.

The company pondered the riddle, while little Stan was "bustin' to tell it."

"One-eyed man?" ventured Jeems.

"You're on the right track."

"Apple tree must work out the same way," I guessed. "Two apples all it had on it?"

"You got it!"

"I don't get it at all," said the same boy.

"One eye ain't *eyes*" sputtered Stan, "and he took *one* apple off and left *one* apple on, and one apple ain't *apples.*"

"I know one," said Steve.

> "I went to the woods and I got it;
> I brought it home because I couldn't find it;
> the more I looked for it the less I liked it,
> and when I did find it, I threw it away."

"Where'd ye learn that 'un?" asked Old Rob. "Hit's a good 'un."

Many guesses were made. "No! — No, that ain't it." And Steve finally had to hint, "Ain't you ever been in the woods barefoot?"

"A tick!" shouted Old Rob.

"Aw, you could find a tick easy, and it wouldn't hurt ye when you looked for it."

"Hit must 'a been a briar," said Old Kel.

"That's right." The boys all went "Aw-w-w!" — and made Steve say it over till they had it by heart.

Jeems spoke up:

> *"I went through a field of wheat;*
> *I saw something good to eat.*
> *It was neither feathers, flesh, nor bone;*
> *I kept it till it walked alone."*

"Ha!" came from Granny. "We know that," said Old Kel.

"Come on, boys," said Jeems.

The boys tried hard, and Jeems at last lent them a hand. "The old hen don't always lay where she ought to."

"A egg!" cried Rhody, beating the boys to it.

More riddles were remembered, told, guessed at, answered, re-told so they could be memorized for stumping others. Coffee was poured for us all, in cups of china and cups of tin. Another green log was brought for the fire and great flames from dry wood were soon leaping over it. Tom sent Steve for more apples.

"I know a man," I said, "who wakes up his apple trees on Old-Christmas Eve."

"Wakes up his apple trees?"

"What about that now!" exclaimed Jeems.

"How did he do it?"

"Everybody goes out in the orchard at sundown and we sing an old song that was handed down for this Apple Tree Wassail — as they call it. And at the end of the song we all shout together:

'Stand fast, root!
Bear well, top!
Every little twig bear an apple big!
Every little bough bear an apple now!
Hats full, caps full, three-bushel bags full,
cellar full, barn floors full,
little heaps under the stairs,
and my pockets full too!'

Then we all set off firecrackers and shotguns, and stomp the ground and whoop and holler as loud as we can."

"A-a-a Lord!" said Old Kel. "Used to be a lot of Old-Christmas signs and ways."

"They used to tell me that alder buds would burst and leaf out on Old-Christmas Eve," said Granny. "Said the bees would roar in the bee-gum like they wanted to swarm."

"Greenbriar will blossom, too," put in Old Kel; "and hop vines spring up."

"Get up on a high place on the twelfth night of Christmas," Granny told us, "and you'll see a big star rise."

"They used to say," murmured Uncle Kel, "that the twenty-fifth was set aside so they could have a big time, celebrate and drink and all. New Christmas was made for man, but Old Christmas — and my grandfather always thought that was the right Christmas — is holy, sacred. You ought to be *good* now, on the twelfth day; not celebrate but stay home and keep that day quiet-like and think on the Lord."

"I used to know a song about the twelve days of Christmas," said Granny, "but hit's done left me, all but the first of it."

"Why, you know that, Tom!" said Rhody. "I heard you singin' it when I went by here the other day. Sing it!"

Tom started the song and Granny said, "That ain't the tune." Tom kept on, and Rhody began to sing parts of it with him. Then Steve joined in, and before the end the whole room was full of singing.

III

O the third day of Christmas my true-love sent to me
three French hens, two turtle doves,
and a parteridge in a pear tree, in a pear tree.

IV

O the fourth day of Christmas my true-love sent to me
four calling birds, three French hens, two turtle doves,
and a parteridge in a pear tree, in a pear tree.

V

O the fifth day of Christmas my true-love sent to me:

O the fifth day of Christmas my true-love sent to me:

five gold - ie wrens, four calling birds,

three French hens, two turtle doves, and a

parteridge in a pear tree, in a pear tree.

[1] Sung to the same phrase as "two turtle doves."
[2] Thus:

four calling birds, three French hens, two turtle doves

VI

O the sixth day of Christmas my true-love sent to me

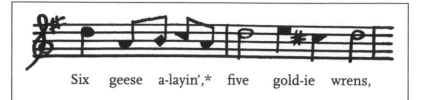

Six geese a-layin',* five gold-ie wrens,

four calling birds, three French hens, two turtle doves,
and a parteridge in a pear tree, in a pear tree.

And so, adding the gifts one by one, we sang on to the last verse:

"O the twelfth day of Christmas my true-love sent to me,
twelve bulls a-bellowin',
eleven lords a-leapin',
ten ladies dancin',
nine boys a-singin',
eight hares a-runnin',
seven swans a-swimmin',
six geese a-layin',
five goldie wrens;
four calling birds,
three French hens,
two turtle doves,
and a parteridge in a pear tree."

Old Kel leaned over to Tom and began to tell him something
Tom's song had reminded him of. I caught the words "seven

---

* The phrase of the tune for this is now used for the rest of the new
gifts — "seven swans a-swimmin'" etc. The new phrase from "five goldie
wrens" back to the "parteridge in a pear tree" is used from now on.

squintin' squirrels, six pippycoritical custards," and I wanted to listen, but Granny London took my ear to tell me where Tom had the song "wrong" both in words and tune.

About the middle of Granny's re-singing there was a burst of laughter from Old Rob and the men and boys listening to Old Kel, so I knew I'd missed something.

Then Tom got up, and took his flashlight down from the fire-board and went out. We heard him turning over boards under the porch. He was brushing snow from his hair and shoulders when he re-entered. "There's your snow, Jeems. Comin' down fast, and stickin' too." The boys were up and out as quick as a wink.

"It's already a inch deep!" one of them called gleefully.

Tom had brought in a long thin piece of board and gone back to work with his knife.

"Tell this man about your huntin' trip, Rob," said Old Kel; "and mind you don't make up no lies." The old man grinned dryly at Jeems and me.

"Why, no, indeed! I might handle the truth just a little careless-like; but I'll tell ye no lies, whole lies, and nothin' but lies." And he put on a most sober face as he started —

ONLY A
FAIR DAY'S HUNTIN'

O ne summer I was workin' in West Virginia, back when I was
young; and a crowd of us boys, off work on a Saturday, we
went to go bathin' in a big pond. Got up there, that pond was
plumb kivvered in wild ducks. Well, I told the other boys to lie low
a minute, slipped off my clothes, grabbed up four plowlines was
layin' there on the fence, and eased in that pond. Slipped under
the water, swum around underneath all them ducks till I'd tied all
their feet up with them lines. Poked my head up amongst 'em,
hollered "Whoo!" and slapped my hands. I had a good grip on the
end of that line and hit tied in one length, but I miscalculated on
how much I could hold, and them ducks got lined up some way
or other and pulled me out the water and flew on off with me a-
hangin' to that plowline. Right on up through the clouds and across
the country they went, and I'd 'a been a goner if I hadn't fin'lly
pulled up a ways on that line and made me a loop. So I slipped
down in that loop and sat there with my legs crossed lookin' over

the country. Houses looked about the size of patent bee-gums, and folks was like ants crawlin' around.

Well, them ducks flew the daylong and right on up in the night, and never showed no sign of givin' out till about sunup Sunday mornin'. So when I see they was headin' down to light, I watched, and time I was on the ground I snubbed the end of that line around a big wahoo. Calculated after I got me a bite to eat somewhere I'd turn their heads and fly 'em back. Went over to a house, was standin' there fairly close, hollered, and a old man come out. Asked him could I get me a little something to eat, and he said yes.

"Anybody there with ye?" I asked him.

"No," he said, "I'm batchin'."

So I come out from behind the bresh and went on to the house.

He handed me a pair of big overalls, says, "The fare'll be pretty bad, but if you can stand it you're welcome."

"Can you tell me where I'm at?" I asked him.

"Why, yes," he says, "you're here."

"Where's here?" I says. "I just come to this country."

"South Carolina," he told me.

"Huntin' good down here?" I asked him.

"Good?" says the old man. "Why, the other day I went out to hunt me a little game—" And that old feller he tried to tell me a lot of stuff that didn't have a bit of truth in it.

So directly we got fixed to go out huntin'. He had an old big-bored gun there, double-barr'led muzzle-loadin' shotgun, and he put a double-charge of powder in both barr'ls—I didn't know he'd done that—loaded her up with buckshot and we headed for the river. 'Course, he let *me* have the gun.

Well, we got down there on the river-bank and looked up the river and there was a big flock of ducks. I raised the gun, but 'fore I could fire I heard a racket down the river, and there was about a hundred wild geese. Well, I wanted the ducks, *and* I wanted them geese, both. So I took a notion: I lowered the gun and stuck the middle finger of each hand in the ends of them gun-barr'ls and pulled 'em apart, bent one to the right and one to the left. Then I raised up and set the gun about level with the water and . . . just as I went to fire a big buck deer slipped down the opposite bank to get him a drink, and I was about to pull that gun straight again so's I could get him instead of the game-birds, but right then a grea-a-t big cottonmouth snake r'ared up out the water and was makin' right at me. —Well, I pulled both triggers.

And that double charge of powder goin' off in both barr'ls at onct, hit kicked me a back somersault up the curve in the bank and threw me right out in the middle of the river. I come back to the top pretty quick and shook the water out my eyes. Seen that old man runnin' downstream to get the dead geese 'fore they floated off; so I stayed out there a-tread-in' water, gathered up my ducks when they floated on down to where I was at. Got holt of 'em and swum on back.

And when I got out on dry land again I felt somethin' floppin' around inside my britches legs, and don't you know that old man's overalls had done run full of fish. Shook myself and there was big catfish come out the right leg, and trout and bass fell out the left 'un. I bent over to pick 'em up, jerked a buckle off one shoulder-strap and hit went flyin' in the grass and killed a big rabbit sittin' there.

Looked around to see what about that snake and it was dead all right. The ramrod had jarred out when I fired, flew straight down that cottonmouth's throat and choked it to death. But I forgot to see what about the deer 'cause just then that old man come back with the geese. So we got to fixin' that gun back straight again, jerked the ramrod out that snake's mouth and put it back in the socket. Then we loaded it — *I* loaded it that time. And when we went to put on the caps we seen both hammers was gone. Just about then we heard a racket, looked across the river and there was that deer backin' against the riverbank and a-dodgin' and a-jumpin' a sound like hornets or somethin' was after it. Well, we swum over right quick, and — don't you know! — them two hammers had that deer hemmed in and cornered and was a-snappin' at it one on one side and the other'n on the other.

So I picked me up a rock and hit the deer between the eyes, grabbed them hammers, and then we floated the deer across, put the hammers back on the gun, picked up all that game and went on back to the old man's shack. He didn't have much to say.

Well, I left him the game: sixty-three ducks, forty-eight geese, twelve big catfish, fifteen trout, four bass weighed about ten or eleven pounds apiece, the deer, and the rabbit. "Only a fair day's huntin'," I told him. "Not bad, but you come on back to Virginia with me and we'll really go on a huntin' trip."

He said no, he didn't reckon he could go right then. So I give him back his overalls and went and turned my string of ducks north. Got fixed in my loop-seat — put me a board in it that time — untied the rope from that wahoo and my ducks took off. We had a good wind with us goin' back, and they landed me right back in that same pond about sundown. I eased out the water with my end of that plowline and looped it over a fencepost right quick. Them ducks was give out but I wasn't takin' no chances on them carryin' me off to Canady or Mexico or some such outlandish place.

Got back in my clothes, and showed up in plenty of time for work on Monday mornin'. — Them ducks got fat bein' tied down to one place like they was, and one Saturday me and the boys had us a big roast-duck picnic up there. I can show ye the place — if you don't believe me.

"Aw, you left out all that about Honey River and Pancake Mountain," complained Steve.

"If I was to try to tell you all that happened on my huntin' trips, boys, we'd be here till tomorrow night too."

Tom had finished the long strip, which he had notched like a saw. He got up and put it on the fireboard with the little man.

"I'd better tell Dick here about the stalk of corn I raised that time," he said.

"Look out, boys!" — and Old Rob ducked as though he were about to be bit. "Tom's goin' to tell a big 'un!"

THE TALL CORNSTALK

Well now, I've seen a lot of things in my time. I remember old Brin, John Edward's big milch cow that gave so much milk, and how she got hung up in a grapevine in a sinkhole out 'side the mountain and how the milk run out of her bag till it filled that hole up over the old cow's head. Drownded her. Yes, sir — and while she was dyin' she kicked around and churned up a hundred pounds of butter. Good butter, too. I eat supper down at John's two years after that and John's old lady had some of it on the table.

And I recollect Johnny Martin's old horse and how he turned him loose in a peavine cove to die when he got too old to work — and anyway, he had them two sores on his back so he couldn't be rode none. Then me and Johnny went huntin' on the ridge above that cove several years after that. Looked off down in the holler, seen a big oak tree a-movin' around down there — and a dogwood follerin' right in behind it. And when we got down there, blamed if it wasn't Johnny's old horse, had them trees growin' up out of him. An acorn had fell in the sore in the middle of his back and a dogwood berry had lodged in the one jest over his hindquarters. And that old horse was spry as a colt. Looked like he got strength from them trees a-takin' root in him like that. Well, Johnny run back home and got his axe, and we cut the oak. I led the old horse out from under it when it fell. Took the horse on in, and Johnny Martin got his adze and his drawknife and some chisels, and he shaped that oak stump into as pretty a saddle as you ever saw. And that dogwood—he never cut it. Jus' left it standin' so's he could have him a shadebush everwhen he had to ride out in the hot sun.

And them snakes that got to fightin'—now I never saw that, but they said both snakes had a holt of each other by the tip of their tails and they both commenced swallerin'. Swallered each other up till there wasn't but about three inches of snake left where one was that much longer'n the other'n.

Yes, and I can remember Gal Swindall's big bull that run around the fodder stack so hard he butted his own rump, butted his brains out.

But anyway, this cornstalk I'm fixin' to tell ye about, hit was the biggest I ever seen. And my two boys, Burl and Blaine, they could prove it to ye if they was here to do it but Burl's in the Hiawathia Islands in the navy and Blaine's in the Marines somewhere over about Chiny.

Well, we was shellin' seed-corn to plant in the old bottom on the creek next to where there used to be an old stave mill where my great-granddaddy's great-great-granddaddy worked. Aimed to have us a good newground for our corn crop that year. I reckon we grubbed a million roots and herbs from that old bottom, besides grapevine and greenbriar and black-berry bresh and grave-yard vine, not to mention trees that had stumps six foot across and locusts thick as wheat in a wheat-field and locusts roots runnin' a mile or so in every direction—and rocks! We could 'a built three hotels out of them rocks we hauled and toted and throwed out of that piece of newground. We had to work awful hard tryin' to make a little somethin' to eat for our family: Mommy and Pa, and Jeb and Ceelie and Deelie (twins, they was) and Tom and Everett and Polly and Matthew and the second set of twins, Allie and Callie, and Hode and Clariebell and the least kids and me and my wife (I was the oldest boy) and my boys Burl and Earl (they was twins, but Earl he died) and Blaine and my three least 'uns—and Grandpa and Grandma and Great-uncle Jeff and Cousin Herman and Cousin Therman (they was twins too) and Aunt Becky (Rebecca —that was her real name) they stayed with us some too back then. Why, I reckon we sweated about ten thousand gallons gettin' that bottom patch cleared and ready for plantin'. And we was pretty peart the day we got through with it: ten acres or more, fine black dirt, level as a housefloor. Well, like I was sayin', we were all out on the back porch shellin' the last of that seed-corn 'fore daylight that mornin', and we was shellin' for a fare-you-well and right then Ma called us to come eat breakfast—when I dropped the ear I had—and I was awful hungry so I left it where it fell off the porch.

And after we'd eat, I looked for it, found where it had fell in the trough where we watered the chickens. Picked it up and right then I noticed where the water had done swelled one of the grains on that cob—swelled it to about the size of a plum. So I shelled the rest of it off and saved that big one to itself. Put it in my pocket.

So we went on down to that field directly and started in plantin'. And about twelve I noticed somethin' bumpin' my leg, seen my pocket bulgin' out like a baseball. That grain of corn had swelled some more. I took it and set it on a big flat rock at the edge of the field. Got all the corn in the ground about sundown, and when I went to get that grain of corn—don't you know!—hit had done swelled to about the size of a big pumpkin. Must 'a weighed about sixty pounds or more. So I called Burl and Blaine and we toted it to one corner of the field, dug us a good-sized hole, and rolled it in.

Shoveled the dirt back over it, stomped it down a lick or two, picked up the shovel and started to go to the house. And we hadn't any more'n turned our backs, when somethin' behind us went off like a shotgun. We jerked around and the stalk of that corn had shot out the ground ten or twelve feet and was a-growin' right on. We watched it a minute or two, and then I run for the axe. I figgered it 'uld take all the strength out the rest of the field. Grabbed the axe up out the chop-block, run back and started cuttin', but that thing was growin' so fast I couldn't hit it twice in the same place. It was gatherin' thick dark about then anyhow so we had to let it grow and went on back to the house.

Sam Morris come over there just as we left the supper-table, and said his mare colt had got out. Asked had we seen her. Told him we hadn't. And when Sam started to leave, I asked him, says, "Sam, did ye ride over?" Said he had. "Where'd ye tie your horse?" "To a big saplin' down there in the corner of your newground." The boys and me went on down there with Sam and I says to him, says, "Is that where ye tied the horse, Sam?"

"Yes," he says. "That's the place all right."

We looked and there wasn't no sign of a horse. Sam had thought that cornstalk was a poplar or somethin'. I told Burl and Blaine to run for the lantern and my old rifle. Flashed the lantern up the stalk and there was the horse about eighty feet off the ground a-hangin' by the bridle. So Blaine held the light and I shot the bridle rein in two, and when the horse fell Sam got on and rode on back home.

Well, in less than three weeks' time that cornstalk was tall as three big poplars. Rest of the corn done all right too. But that tall cornstalk wasn't like no other you ever seen. Sprouted a pretty big ear for every blade. You could see 'em start out everwhen the blades unquiled their full length, generally about a hundred foot from the ground. Slowed up some when the rest of the corn tosseled out and commenced silkin'. Didn't grow but about a foot a minute

for several weeks and fin'lly, about corn-cuttin' time, it stopped. You couldn't see the tossel on it even with a spyglass.

Well, we got the little corn cut in about a couple of days. Then we borryed a few axes and started in on that tall cornstalk. Took me and Uncle Jeff and grandpaw and Jeb and Everett and Tom and Matthew and Herman and Therman all day, and about sundown it started fallin'. We watched it fall a while but it got plumb thick dark 'fore it had fell all the way. — Heard it hit the ground about midnight. Made a pretty big racket — even woke up Uncle Jeff.

So early next mornin' we walked up in the pasture-field on the hill behind the barn to see which-a-way it had fell. Hit lay across the creek, over Flint Austin's place, 'cross the top of old Frankie Shacklebrain's big house, and we could see it must 'a crossed the hard-surface road. So we got in the truck and drove on over there. Seen it there above the telephone wires and stretched across a thick woods north side the road. Well, we took out west till we got to Highway 25, and when we crossed Clinch River we could see it was headed for the mountains. So we drove on through the low country, crossed Powell River, and — don't you know! — directly we come on a string of automobiles and wagons ahead of us and they told us there was a big corn tossel layin' in The Cumberland Gap — right in three forks of the highway, had the traffic backed up forty miles in Tennessee, Kentucky, and Virginia. So we turned the trucks around and headed back home.

Well, boys, livestock and folks lived good off our cornstalk all through that section of the country. What fodder we 'uns gathered up, hit filled the barn loft plumb to the rafters; and we had three big shocks out in the pasture, ever' shock twice as big as the barn. And out of what'n-all we gathered, we sold the other half.

Well — we gathered that corn with teams and log-grabs — one ear at a time. Rolled it up with canthooks, piled it high as we could, and sent off for a circus tent to pull over it and keep the rain off. Didn't take but two grains of that corn to make a bushel of meal, but you had to bust it with an axe and take it by the rock-crusher 'fore it 'uld go in the hopper at the mill.

We didn't mind lettin' anybody have some of our corn, but we gathered all we could as far as Tazewell, and there was one great big ear we wanted bad, but hit was stuck in the ground. When that stalk fell this one big ear had mired straight down, small end foremost, in a new-plowed field. We dug around it and tried ever' way in the world to get it out and Burl rigged him up a kind of derrick out of the forks of a tree and a thick chestnut pole, and we got grabs in the end of the cob. (It was mired deep and we jest could knock the grabs in place.) Then we hitched a team to the lower end of that pole and they pulled hard but they couldn't budge it. So we got another team but they didn't help much. So directly we had six teams lined up, and when they fin'lly give a good pull all together — don't you know! — they jerked the cob out. Left a forty-foot well already rocked up.

Hit gave good water, that well did — all that fall and winter and spring, but way along late the next summer, July and August, the weather was awful hot and that corn got to fermentin', and about September first you couldn't draw a thing out of that well but puore mash.

Uncle Jeff he had him a little still then, back in a holler and he run off several thousand gallons of it 'fore winter set in. Made pretty good likker too. Jest a little small dram of it made you feel high as that cornstalk was 'fore we cut it down.

Granny had been chuckling to herself as Tom's tale was ending. "Kel," she said, "you better tell Old Roaney just to make these fellers hush."

"He's been waitin' out on us," grinned Old Rob. "'Tain't no use, boys! We might as well 'a not started."

Old Kel pulled a long face and told —

OLD ROANEY

One time there was an old man lived on yonder side of the mountain. He was an awful hand to hunt, hunted all the time, never *had* follered nothin' but huntin'. Him and his old woman they lived mostly on wild meat. 'Course they had to buy a little meal and coffee and sech. And this was back in old times when it was pretty thin-settled in here, and the settlement (that's where the store was at), hit was plumb the other side of the mountain.

Well, one cold winter mornin' the old lady raised up from where she was a-cookin' in the fireplace, says, "Old man, we done run plumb out of salt. I told you last week that salt-gourd was rattlin' mighty holler. And besides that, there hain't a scrap of meal left, and I cooked up the very last ground of coffee for your breakfast this mornin', and we're low on sugar, and I scraped on the bottom of the flour barr'l last night when I made up your biscuits. You done let us run out of rations. Now you saddle your old pack-mare and git on over that mountain or we'll be eatin' nothin' but unsalted meat."

"Well," says the old man, "I'll be goin' out in a day or two, I reckon. Hit's a-snowin' pretty bad right now."

"You git Old Roaney and fetch us in some rations *today*, old man. You can eat wild meat with no salt and no bread if you want, but I ain't a-goin' to stand for no sech a thing. Git out of here now and go on to the store like I tell ye."

"Well," he says, "I'll go directly."

That old man he wasn't even studyin' about makin' ar' trip out to the settle-ment, cold as it was; but when he went to fill up his powder horn, his last keg of powder had jest a little bitty dribble in it. "Blame!" he says, "I can't fetch in much game with that." He *had* to go to the store now.

So he pulled his old coonskin hat down over his ears, opened the door-shutter, hollered "Roaney!", whistled a couple of times. Old Roaney nickered and directly here she come a-trompin' through the snow. She 'uz an awful good old mare. Come on to the house and stood there to see what did the old man want. So he give her a peck of oats. (Only crop the old man ever did raise. Had him a little deadened patch of newground in the bottoms where he put in a few oats ever' year for his old mare. He didn't like farmin'; didn't like to foller *nothin'* but huntin' and a little fishin' ever' now and then.) So he took the saddle off the wall and throwed hit on Old Roaney. Waited for her to git done mommickin' her oats. Then he bridled her and tied on a few furs he had saved up, jumped in the saddle and hunkered down in his coat collar, and give Old Roaney her head. She 'uz a good old mare. She knowed it was about time to go out and pack in some rations and ammunition. So she took the old man right on over the mountain and on down to the settle-ment. Hit was a right far piece.

So when Old Roaney fin'lly stopped, the old man knowed she was at the store. Stuck his head up out of his old coat, grabbed up his bundle of furs and jumped off and run on in, throwed the furs down on the counter and started in tradin'. Well, he got eight bushels of meal and eight big tins of bakin' sody, a two-hundred-pound sack of tree sugar, hundred pounds of green coffee (that was back in old times when you had to roast it and grind it at home), three two-bushel pokes of wheat-flour, fifty-pound poke of salt, twelve fifty-pound kegs of powder, several dozen bars of lead (had to mold your own bullets back then; muzzle-loadin' hog-rifles was all they had to shoot with), got himself twenty-four dozen twists of tobacco, and several little ar-ticles for his wife. Took all that out and packed it on his old mare. Crawled up in the saddle, says, "Git-up, Roaney." And Old Roaney started on off toward the mountain.

Now, the old man had him a few balls left in his shot-pouch, and he'd done tapped the bung in one of them kegs of powder and filled up his powder horn, so he had his gun ready to fire. (The old folks they *al*-ways kept their old hog-rifles ready-loaded to shoot.) And when they got on up in the mountain he looked out and seen a big buck deer standin' up the slope a little piece. Upped with his rifle-gun . . . BAM! . . . and down come the deer. Went and got it, dragged it out in the trail, skinned him a strop of rawhide off one of its legs, tied its feet together, heaved it up and hung it on the saddle horn. Got back in the saddle and on they went. Looked out before him directly and here come a great big old black bear a-shummickin' right down the middle of the trail. "If I can jest git you now, your fat'll season my buck." (Well, the old folks *always* kept their long-rifles ready-loaded.) So he upped with the muzzle, squeezed the trigger, and at the crack of the gun down come the bear. Hit 'uz a big 'un too. The old man dragged it down on the uphill side of the trail, prized it up on a log was layin' there about level with the old mare's back, got its feet tied up, pulled Old Roaney over to that log and hooked the bear's feet over the saddle-horn. Got back in the saddle — "Git-up, Roaney" — and Old Roaney started easin' away from that log. Now, when that bear's weight pulled off the log and struck Old Roaney she stopped and turned her head and looked back at the old man. But she was an awful good old mare: she stretched out and shifted her fore feet, put her old head down and shifted her hind feet, and picked her way up the mountain.

When they got up in the gap the old man thought he 'uld let her blow a spell 'fore he started down. And while he was a-waitin' he heard a dove moanin' right close; looked out before him and seen it sittin' on a dead limb right over the trail. Well, he thought he'd take his old woman a little bait of fresh bird-meat for her supper. So he upped with his old rifle-gun (the old folks never did fail to keep their guns ready-loaded), and he took that dove right in the head. It fell and caught in the bresh 'side the trail, so directly he pulled on over there and reached down out the saddle to pick it up. And — don't you know! — time he took holt on that dove, little as it was, Old Roaney scooched down and her back give away. Still, she 'uz an awful good old mare. She always done the best she could: she kept her head up and her rump up, but her old belly swagged on the ground. So the old man jumped off of her, seen the shape she was in, says, "Now I declare! I believe Old Roaney's back's done gone and broke. Now, what'n the nation will I do?"

Well, he unloaded her but she still couldn't heave herself off'n the ground; so the old man jest knowed her back was broke, and he got to studyin' what to do. So he split Old Roaney down the forehead, and cut her around the hocks, and then he slipped up behind her with a two-handed bresh — and come at her hollerin' and swarped her good — and it scared her so she jumped right out of her skin.

So then the old man took Old Roaney's skin and stretched it out on the ground, put them rations and all that plunder in it, and the deer and the bear and the dove, and tied the four legs across, got his head up through it where he'd left it tied jest right, took holt on a little dogwood tree and pulled up, swung that load around on his back and put out down the mountain.

Well, he got in home, jerked open the door-shutter, and went on in the house. Now, he'd forgot his pipe when he went out and he was wantin' a smoke awful bad. So he walked over to the fireplace, got his old cob pipe down off the fire-board, crumbled some tobacco in it, scooped him up a coal of fire and got it lit. Started in walkin' the floor, a-smokin' and a-worryin' about his old pack-mare.

He thought the world of Old Roaney. Well, he tromped backerds and forrads a spell, a-smokin' and a-worryin', and directly his old woman raised up, looked at him, says, "Old man, why in the nation don't you lay that pack down and go get washed for supper?"

So the old man he slung his pack off on the floor and untied it. Piled them rations in one corner, put his powder in a good dry place, throwed the bars of lead down one side the hearthrock, laid his tobacco on one end of the fireboard and his wife's stuff on the other, skun out the deer and the bear and took the meat on out and hung it up, picked and cleaned that dove and handed it to his old lady. Then he took the deer-skin and the bear-skin and Old Roaney's hide and throwed them down behind the door where he kept all his skins and sech. So him and the old woman they eat supper and went on to bed.

Well, 'way up in the night the old lady woke up, punched her old man, says, "Get up, old man, and see what that is pawin' at the door. Sounds like Old Roaney, sure's the world!"

"Old Roaney — the nation! Old Roaney's up there on top of the mountain with her back broke and no hide on her. Go on back to sleep, old woman."

The old lady she tried to go to sleep but she couldn't. And directly she heard it again: pawin', pawin'. So she gouged the old man with her elbow, says, "Old man, you get up now and go see what that is. Sounds pint blank like Old Roaney, the way she does everwhen you forget to feed her and she comes a-pawin' at the door after ye."

"I done told ye, old woman! Old Roaney's up there on the mountain with her back broke plumb in two and her hide a-layin' there behind the door. Now, you hush up and quit botherin' me."

So the old man he rolled over and commenced snorin'; but the old lady couldn't get to sleep and couldn't get to sleep, and then she heard it again — pawin', pawin', pawin' like it 'uld break down the doorstep; and that time it nickered. So she raised up and jerked the covers off the old man, set in to punchin' him and shakin' him till she got him woke up, says, "Now you get right out of this bed, old man, and go see what that is. I heard it nicker jest now, and I tell ye hit *is* Old Roaney. You git your britches on and go yonder and open that door, or I'll not give ye no more peace the rest of this night."

"Old woman, you're crazy as a betsy-bug! Hit's a heifer plunderin' around out there, or some other brute done broke loose from somewhere. Well, jest to pacify ye, I'll have to show you hit ain't Old Roaney."

So the old man he crawled out. Put a chunk of lightwood on the fire and when it flared up he went and opened the door; and Old Roaney stuck her head in the house. There she was, the cold snow a-foggin' and a-pilin' down on her, and her jest a-shakin' and a-shiverin' with no hide to her back. So the old man he reached down behind the door right quick to get her skin and put it back on her. Got out there tryin' to get it stretched out to cover her and it didn't seem to go jest right. Well, he 'lowed he'd have to tie it on, but he didn't have no hickory bark twists handy, so he reached over close to the house where he knowed some blackberry bushes was at, broke him off a handful and wrenched 'em and twisted 'em till he'd fixed him up a withe. Tied the skin on his old mare with that withe. Went on back and jumped in the bed. Old Roaney didn't bother 'em no more, and him and the old woman slept right on.

Well, the next mornin' when it got daylight enough the old man looked out to see about his old pack-mare — and he seen what a bobble he'd made. He'd killed a big buck sheep a couple of days before, and instead of gettin' Old Roaney's hide he had grabbed up that sheep-skin and tied hit on her. He went out and tried to pull it off, and — don't you know! — hit had done took root and wouldn't come. So he jest left it, and hit growed right on. Covered her bodaciously all over in jest a very few weeks. Growed down her legs and underneath her, wool patches on her head, and the

biggest sheep-tail you ever seen a-hangin' down behind. And they tell me the old man sheared her twicet a year. Got more wool off Old Roaney than forty head of sheep. Peart too, but she *was* sorty sway-backed the rest of her days.

And I have heard it told how that blackberry withe took root around her like a bellyband. And the old woman never did have to go out in the bresh no more after her blackberries. When blackberry time come she 'uld jest call Old Roaney and pick blackberries off her sides — got enough to make several pies, ever' pickin'. But I'll jest tell ye now. I never did really believe *that* part of the tale.

"Hand him the cake! He's took it!" And Big Rob laughed till he nearly bounced out of his chair.

Harry slapped his knees and laughed till his eyes watered. "Uncle Kel, I been knowin' you ever since I was a little chap. Why in the nation ain't you never told me that tale before this?"

"You never asked me."

"I just recollected one," said Granny, "about an old woman and some rogues."

OLD ONE-EYE

One time there was a rich old lady, lived all by herself. She had a lot of money; kept it right in the house on the fireboard. And every evenin' she 'uld sit by the fire and card wool. Had her a big dried fish hangin' up one side the fireplace and that fish didn't have but one eye, so the old lady called it "One-Eye." Well, she 'uld sit and card wool of an evenin' till she gaped three times, then she'd eat her a piece of that fish and go on to bed.

Now there were three rogues come into that settle-ment and they heard somebody tellin' how that old lady kept all her money at home on the fireboard, so they decided they'd rob her. The big robber he didn't have but one eye. And he made a plan to watch the old lady till she went to bed; so he sent one rogue to hide in the chimney corner and watch. The man went and got up close to the house and looked through a crack in the logs right there by the chimney. Heard the old lady's cards a-goin' "Scratch! scratch! scratch!" So he waited and watched and listened.

The old lady she carded a while then she stopped and stretched and gaped, says, "That's one come." Says, "Two more and then I'll get out my knife." And she looked over at her old dried fish. Hit was hangin' on the same side the fireplace, where the rogue was peepin' through the crack, and he thought she was lookin' right square at him. So when he heard her talkin' about two more to come and gettin' out her knife, he run back and told the other rogues she was a witch. The one-eyed 'un didn't believe him. Sent the other man to watch.

So he got there in the chimney corner and about the time he looked through the crack the old lady raised her head and gaped again, says, "That's two come. One more and I'll get my butcher knife." Looked over at her fish. And that rogue put out from there quick. Ran back and told the one-eyed rogue he was sure that old woman was a witch. Said, "Let's not rob her. She'll git us with her butcher knife sure's the world!"

So the big one-eyed rogue he had to go and watch. He looked through the crack and seen the old lady cardin', cardin', cardin', and rockin' in her chair, and directly she stopped and gaped real big, set her wool-cards on the table, says, "Aa, Lord! That's the third. And now, Old One-Eye, I'm goin' to cut me a chunk out of you." And she grabbed up her butcher knife and made for that dried fish.

Well, that one-eyed rogue jumped out of the chimney corner and run for life, and him and his two buddies left that country in a hurry.

And the old rich lady she cut her off a piece of that fish and eat it, and went on to bed and slept sound.

NEARLY DAYLIGHT

One of the little boys had wakened, slipped off the bed, and climbed up in Old Robin's lap. He broke the silence that had followed our laughter over Old One-Eye with a small drowsy voice.

"Rob?"

"What, son?"

"Sing 'Froggy-went-a-courtin'-he-did-ride.'"

Rhody reached over the foot of the bed and shook one of the little girls. "Wake up if you want to hear 'Miss Mousie.'" The child sat up, rubbed her eyes, slid to the floor and wobbled a bit unsteadily toward the fireplace. Delia took her on her lap and stroked her towsled head.

As Old Robin began to sing the other little boy on the bed woke up, and was soon nestled in Tom's arms. And before the fourth verse every young 'un on the big bed had wakened as if by magic and crept into some grown-up's lap.

FROGGY WENT A-COURTIN'

Froggy went a-courtin' and he did ride — unk!
Froggy went a-courtin' and he did ride
With a sword and pistol by his side —
A-kiddely waddely, kiddely waddely, unk, unk, unk!
He rode down to Miss Mousie's door,

where he'd often been before.
Little Miss Mousie came tripping down,
in her velvet satin gown.
Then Miss Mousie asked him in
where she sat to card and spin.
He took Miss Mousie on his knee,
said, Miss Mousie, will you marry me?
Without my Uncle Rat's consent
I would not marry the pres-i-dent.
Soon Uncle Rat came home:
Who's been here since I been gone?
Nice young man with a moustache on,
a-askin' me to marry him.
O Uncle Rat gave his consent,
so they were married and away they went.
O where will the wedding supper be?
Away down yonder in a holler tree.
O what will the wedding supper be?
Two butterbeans and a black-eyed pea.
O the first to come in was a little white moth,
spreading down the table cloth.
O the next to come in was a bumblebee,
set his banjo on his knee.
O the next to come in was a nimble flea,
took a jig with the bumblebee.
O the next to come in was two little ants,
a-fixin' around to have a dance.
O the next to come in was the old gray goose,
she picked up her fiddle, and she cut loose!
O the next to come in was the old red cow,
she tried to dance but she didn't know how.
O the next to come in was the betsey-bug,
passin' around the cider jug.

The next to come in was the old grey cat
said she'd put an end to that.
The bride went scramblin' up the wall,
she let out an awful squall.
Froggy went swimmin' across the lake,
he got swallered by a big black snake.
The song book's sittin' on the shelf, um-hum!
The song book's sittin' on the shelf,
if you want any more you can sing it yourself!

FROGGY WENT A-COURTIN'

Froggy went a-courtin' and he did ride — unk!

Froggy went a — courtin' and he did ride

With a sword and pistol by his side —

A - kiddely waddely, kiddely waddely, unk, unk, unk!

Tom lifted his lap-sitter over and
propped him on Rob's other knee. Then
he took the little man and the notched
stick down from the fireboard. "Stan,
go find me a rock about the size of both
your fists. Here," and he handed him the
flashlight. While Stan hunted the
rock, Tom looped a length of string
about the little man's neck, fastened
it someway to the saw, inserted the
top of the saw between the gripping
hands, and tied another string to the
bottom end of the saw. Stan brought the
rock. The children were watching every
move. The rock was tied to the lower end
of the saw, and Tom set the little man's feet
on the edge of the mantel. The rock swung
free and Tom gave it a gentle push.

Leaning way over the edge the little carved
man began to saw. And all the kids were wide-
eyed.

"Stand back, boys, so we can all see."

"Aw! Look!"

"What keeps him from fallin' off?"

"Can I have it, Tom?"

"I want me one, too!"

"You boys can all make you one. I'll help ye
get started."

Every boy had a good look at the little
saw-man and a try at making it work.

"I'm goin' to start me one right now,"
said Steve.

The little man kept sawing away, and

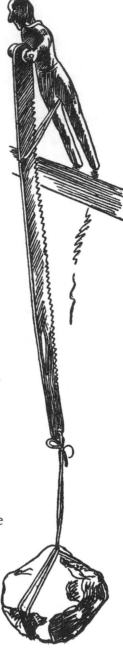

when the rock's momentum played out some boy's hand reached up and gave it another easy push. Delia was rocking her chair and humming low to the child in her lap. The last of the pile of wood went on the fire. And Big Rob took over.

"One more tale, and then you kids better go home and get some sleep. Good thing tomorrow's Sunday!"

And he told —

THE GREEN GOURD

One time there was an old woman lived all by herself in the head of a holler. And one day this old woman went to the spring after a bucket of water, and she dropped her gourd-dipper and broke it. She *had* to have a dipper, so she went to look at the gourdvine she had out on the fence. It had some big dipper gourds a-hangin' on it but there wasn't none of 'em ripe. Well, the old folks always said you oughtn't never to pull a green gourd. Said was you to pull a gourd 'fore it was plumb dry-ripe, it 'uld witch ye sure. But this old woman she was in a hurry about her dipper, so she said, "Humpf! I'll pull me a green gourd if I want to!" — and she went right straight and jerked one off.

Took it on in the house, put it up on the fireboard to dry. Then she went on about her business. Well, she was sittin' there knittin' when that green gourd rolled off from up there, hit the hearthrock — Fump! The old lady picked it up and put it back. Then she stooped over to mend her fire and that green gourd rolled off again, bounced on the floor — Fump! Fump!

"O yes, you ain't a-goin' to stay up there, are ye? Well, I'll just see about that!" And she propped that green gourd 'way back on the fireboard with a big stick of kindlin'. Sat down again with her knittin' when all at once the green gourd raised up from behind that chunk of kindlin', drawed back and slammed right down the middle of the fireboard, knocked the clock off and scattered the bottles and papers every which-a-way, jumped off and sailed around in the house, knocked over some chairs, and then it made for that old woman and commenced fumpin' her right in the back of the head — Fump! Fump! Fump!

Well, that old lady she'd done already headed for the door but time that green gourd lammed her, she picked up her skirts and put out. Out the door she flew and took out down the holler just a-squallin' and that green gourd jumpin' right in behind her. She'd outrun it part the time, but it 'uld catch up with her, fump her again, and she'd bawl and duck and run right on.

Got down the holler a piece, came to the groundhog's house. The old groundhog was sittin' there by the door, saw her comin', says, "What's the matter, old woman?"

"O law!" she says, "this green gourd's after me!"

"Run in here. I'll get after *it*."

So she ran in the groundhog's house, got down behind the door. The green gourd bounced right on in the house after her, and when the groundhog made a pass at it, hit knocked that old groundhog's legs out from under him, fumped him in the ribs a time or two, drawed back and slammed him right on the end of his nose, knocked him a back somersault, sailed around behind the door and fumped the old lady. She hollered and out the door she put.

"Oo-oo law! I got to get shet of this green gourd!"

On down the holler she ran. Came to the fox's house. The fox was sittin' there by the door, says, "What's the matter, old lady?"

"O law! This green gourd's tryin' to witch me!"

"Run in here. I'll witch *it*!"

So she ran in the fox's house and got down behind the door. Here came the green gourd! The old fox snapped at it, and it raised up and lammed him right on the top of the head, knocked him down. Sailed in behind the door and fumped the old woman. Out the door she went!

"Oo-oo law! I got to get shet of this green gourd!"

On down the holler! Came to the wildcat's house. He was sittin' outside, says, "What's the matter, old woman?"

"O law! This green gourd's about to run me to death!"

"Run in here. Hit won't get past me!"

In she ran, got down behind the door. Here came the green gourd a-rollin' and a-bouncin'. The wildcat jumped for it and it turned back and smacked that old cat right square between the eyes, knocked him sprawlin'. Fumped the old woman. Out she hopped and on down the holler!

"Oo-oo-oo law! Got to get shet of this green gourd!"

Came to the pant'er's house. He was stretched out by the door, raised up, says, "What's the matter, old woman?"

"O law! Hit's this green gourd! Hit'll have me kilt yet!"

"Run in here. *I'll* handle it!"

She ran on in behind the door, and that green gourd sailed right in after her. The pant'er jumped at it, scratched it a little, bit a chunk out of it. Then the green gourd it stopped and let go again — and punched the old pant'er right smack in the belly, knocked the wind out of him. Sailed in around behind the door, came down on the old woman — fumped her right on.

"Oo-oo-oo-oo law! Got — get shet — this green gourd!" She went a-tearin' on down the holler and that green gourd was just a-rattlin' on her. She ran with all her might and outran it a good piece that time. Came to the bear's house. The old bear was standin' r'ared up in the door, says, "WHAT'S THE MATTER, OLD WOMAN?"

"O law!" she says, and she was out of breath, "This green gourd

— hit's just about got me! I've tried to hide — behind everybody's front door — all the way — down the holler! And yonder it comes again! O law!"

"RUN IN HERE, OLD WOMAN. *I'LL* GIVE IT GREEN GOURD!"

She ran in the bear's house, and got down behind the door, but the old bear came and nosed her out.

"LET ME GET THERE, OLD LADY. YOU HIDE IN HERE."

And he shoved the old woman in his clothes-closet, and slipped behind the door right quick.

Well, that green gourd shot in the house, sailed in behind the door and — the old bear he turned around quick and sat on it: squnched it all to pieces.

The old woman she was so glad to get shet of the green gourd

she just laughed and hollered. Then she took the broom and swept it in the fireplace and burnt it up.

"Much obliged," she says to the old bear. "Now hain't there somethin' I can do for you?"

"WELL, A LITTLE BAIT OF HONEY SHORE WOULD TASTE GOOD."

"Come on," says the old woman.

She and the bear went on back to the pant'er's house.

"Much obliged for tryin' to help me like you done. Now what can I do to help you?"

"Well now," says the pant'er, "I'd ruther like to have me a pig."

"Come on," she told him.

They went on to the wildcat's house. The old woman thanked the wildcat and asked him what he 'uld like to have.

"Chickens," says the wildcat.

"Come on."

Got to the fox's house.

"I sure do thank you for tryin' to help me. What can I do for you now?"

"Well," says the fox, "I'd not mind if I had me a couple of ducks — fat 'uns."

"Come on with us."

They got up there to the groundhog's place and there wasn't nobody in sight. So they hollered a couple of times and directly the old groundhog came to the door a-limpin' and holdin' on to his sides, and had his nose all wropped up in a piece of rag.

"I'm mighty much obliged to ye," says the old lady, "for tryin' to help me. Now you tell me what I can do to help you."

"Well, bab," says the groundhog, "a bess of tirdips 'uld be bighty dice."

"Come on."

So she took 'em all on back down to the mouth of the holler and out in the bottoms and on to where an old stingy farmer lived at.

The old woman she knowed he'd gone off to town that day, and there wasn't nobody at home but the dog. So when they all got to the fence the old woman stopped, says, "Now you 'uns jest stand over there and wait a minute." Then she stooped over and raised up the bottom fence-rail, put her fingers in her mouth and whistled right sharp. The old dog came lopin' out from the house, and when he saw all them varmints at the fence he just made for 'em—

"A-woo! Woo! WOO-OO!"

and when he tried to scrouge under the fence the old lady she dropped the rail on his neck, and that held him. So they let the old dog howl, and they all started gettin' over the fence.

The old woman she pulled off a couple of top-rails, h'isted one side of her skirts, and she got over all right. The old bear just stood up and put his front paws down on the other side and humped himself, and he got over. The pant'er he hunkered back and jumped —and there he was. The wildcat crawled up one side and jumped off the top rail. And the fox put up his forefeet and he clambered over. The old groundhog he kept tryin' to find him some hole or other to crawl through, and tryin' not to get too close to that dog, and fin'lly the old bear went back and reached and scooped him up easy with one paw and set him over.

So then they all scattered to get what they'd come for, and the old woman she watched out for the old farmer if he was to come back. Then directly here came the old bear a-grinnin' and a-huggin' a big tub of honey, and his jaws just a-dribblin'. The pant'er came back with a shoat under his arm and hit a-squealin' every breath. The wildcat had him about a dozen chickens with their legs tied up. And the fox came with fat ducks under both arms. And they waited and waited for the groundhog, and fin'lly here he came draggin' a big poke of turnips—and the poke three times bigger'n he was. He was havin' a time, so the old woman she went and holp him.

And when the groundhog and her got to the fence the others had all got over — all but the old bear; he was a-waitin', says, "HOLD THIS FOR ME, PLEASE, MA'M, WHILST I GET OVER."

So he humped over the fence and then the old lady handed him his tub of honey, and then them turnips. Then she picked up the groundhog and set him over the fence, h'isted her skirts and *she* got over.

So they all went back up the holler and stopped off where they lived at, and the old woman she holp the groundhog plumb to his door with all that big mess of turnips.

Then she went on to her little place up in the head of the holler — and they tell me she never did pull another green gourd as long as she lived.

Old Rob paused, then quite suddenly he picked up the tale again.

"The old woman had run so hard the sole of one of her shoes had come loose. So first thing when she got home again, she jerked that shoe off and got her some stout thread and waxed it, then she took that little thing with a sharp point — what-ye-call-it — you know: that sharp thing in a little handle, what you punch holes in leather with — "

"A awl," said Stan.

"That's *all*!" shouted Old Rob, and the boys had a good laugh at Stan for being caught.

"Go on home now, all of ye! Wake! Awake! Day's a-goin' to break!"

The young 'uns stretched and relaxed again, reluctant to summon their energies for rising and departing. The two windows were graying with a hint of dawn. The lamp's oil was almost out again and I had scratched out the last of "Green Gourd" by twisting around and writing by firelight.

Harry and the other father who had joined us got up, and Rhody spoke out.

"You ain't told 'Chunk o' Meat.'"

"Why, honey, you've heard that a thousand times," protested Granny.

"Let Rob tell it!"

"Rob, you tell it!"

"Ain't goin' to do it," teased Old Rob.

"Tell it! I bet that man ain't never heard it. Tell it to *him*."

"Aw, I reckon he knows it already."

I did know it but I didn't let on. And after a bit more pleading and teasing, Old Rob started —

The two children slipped off Big Rob's lap and leaned against Delia's chair, looking at me while the tale progressed, and giggling with delight as Rob drew near the ending.

CHUNK O' MEAT

One time there was a little old man and a little old woman and a little old boy. And one evenin' they were all out in the garden pickin' beans for supper; and they didn't have no meat to put in the beans. Well, they picked and picked and the little old woman she got her little tin bucket full, so she went on back to the house. Then the little old man he got his little tin bucket full and he went on back to the house. Well, the little old boy he fooled around and fooled around and his little tin bucket hit wasn't even half full. He picked along and picked along, just piddlin' and playin' in the dirt half the time, and he kept studyin' about no meat to put in the beans.

Well, he got to pickin' on a beanvine that ran along the top of an old holler log there on the back side of the garden — picked along, picked along till he came to the big end of that holler log. And there, right in the mouth of the holler, was a nice chunk of fat-meat. That little old boy he set down his little tin bucket, and picked up the chunk of meat. Then two big eyes opened up and looked out from 'way back in the holler log and that little old boy he snatched up his little tin bucket and made for the house — a-whippity-cut! — right down the middle of the garden a-knockin' beanpoles and cornstalks every which-a-way. Ran in the house and shut the door right quick. And the little old woman she took his little tin bucket and fussed at him for havin' it not even half full. Then they all sat down and commenced breakin' and stringin' the beans.

Well, the little old boy he kept that chunk of meat in his hand and directly he slipped out and washed it right quick in the wash basin on the back porch, slipped back in the house. And the little old woman she fussed at him for slippin' out. And directly they got the beans all broke and strung.

So then the little old man he went out after a turn of firewood and the little old woman she hung the pot in the fireplace, poured in some water and dumped in the beans. And the little old boy he slipped over to the fireplace and waited till the old woman had her back turned settin' the table and then he slipped up the potlid right quick and popped that chunk of meat in with the beans.

Well, the little old man got the wood all cut and he brought it in and throwed it down by the hearthrock, and then he sat down one side the fire to wait for the beans to cook. And the little old woman she got the table all set and she drawed her up a chair and sat down the other side the fire to wait for the beans to cook. And the little old boy he sat down right in the middle of the hearth-rock and doubled his legs up under him. And they waited and waited and directly the beans got done. So the little old woman she scooped up a mess of beans and they all went to the table and got 'em a bait of beans and started in eatin'.

The little old man tasted his beans, says, "Mm! Meat!" Then the little old woman she tasted hers, says, "Mm! Meat!" The little old boy tasted his, didn't say nothin'.

Well, they got done eatin' and sat down by the fire again, and directly they heard somethin' comin' away off, says, "Where's my chunk of me-e-eat?"

The little old woman she jumped up and went and got under the bed.

The little old man and the little old boy sat right on and then they heard it again — comin' closer — "Where's my chunk of me-e-eat?"

And the little old man he ran and got under the bed.

The little old boy he sat right on, kind of scared and kind of sleepy, and then he heard the gate-chain rattle.

"Where's my chunk of me-e-eat?"

Heard somethin' climbin' up on the porch-roof.

"Where's my chunk of me-e-e-eat?"

Then he heard it clawin' on the house-roof.

"*Where's my chunk of me-e-e-eat?*"

Then he heard somethin' scratchin' in the chimney. Saw soot falling, looked up the chimney, and up there on the smoke-shelf sat a great — big — old — black — hairy — booger,

"WHERE'S MY CHUNK O' MEAT?"

The little old boy he was so scared by then he couldn't move.

"W-w-w-what you got sech big eyes for?"

> "*Stare you through!*
> *Stare you thro-o-o-ough!*"

"W-w-w-w-what you got sech big claws for?"

> "*Grabble your grave!*
> *G-r-r-rabble — your gra-a-a-ave!*"

"W-w-w-w-w-what you got sech a bushy tail for?"

> "*Sweep your grave!*
> *Sweep — your — gra-a-a-a-ave!*"

"W-w-w-w-w-w-what you got sech long, sharp snaggly teeth for?"

"*EAT YOU UP!*"

Old Rob had gradually edged his chair around toward me, and at "Eat you up!" had jumped straight for me. I gasped and grabbed at the edge of the oak chest as my chair went over backwards, and there was a great shout from the children.

Amidst the laughter the two fathers rose. "Come on, you kids, or you'll be late for Sunday school. Get your coats on."

Someone opened the door, and the room flashed with a bright glare.

"It's done stopped snowin'."

Everybody filed out to see the snow. The sun was just below the horizon, the eastern sky clear under a long ledge of gray, and cloud-reflected light filtered out over a white world.

"Come go home with us."

"Can't go. You 'uns stay and eat breakfast."

"We'll have to get on in home now."

"Well, come to see us."

"All right. You 'uns come."

"Come whenever you're a mind to."

"I'll come."

"We'll be a-lookin' for ye."

The usual parting phrases were repeated as each group made tracks across the snow. And finally there were only the Weavers, Tom, Jeems, and I left in the house. Delia and Sarah were starting a fire in the kitchen cook-stove. Steve and Stan laid themselves across Tom's bed and slept. Big Rob and Tom dozed in their chairs. Little Rob was out at the woodpile chopping fuel for the breakfast fire. Old Kel was poking chunks together with one of his walking sticks. Granny turned to me.

"You takin' down the old songs, too?"

"Yes'm. I've been after songs longer than I have tales."

"Tom — *Tom!* — Get that old hymn book, the one that was your mother's."

Tom got up and went and rummaged in his trunk and brought out the book.

"Hit's the old 'Southern Harmony,'" said Granny. "We got one at home and we get it out every now and then, set it on the table when we've cleared away supper — sing all the parts."

I came and looked over Granny's shoulder. It was an aged book, opening longways; tattered at the edges, its back broken and the board covers loose. Granny fingered the yellow pages.

"Here's one," she said, "that we know to sing."

I bent closer and read its title: "The Babe of Bethlehem." There were three staves, and the note-heads were square and round and diamond-shaped, and one was like a little pennant.

"Hit's fa-sol-la singin'," explained Granny. "Deely she knows the tribble, and Rob the bass. Kel and me, we generally hold the tenor. — Rob! Wake up. Come in here, Deely."

Rob woke up; Delia came and sat by Granny London.

"Law, faw, law, law, law, faw, law," sang Granny.

"That's too high," said Old Rob. "You pitch it, Deely."

Delia tried the pitch, and the quartet tried it with her: "Law, do, mi, law, mi, do, law."

Old Rob nodded, and quietly they began to sing:

THE BABE OF BETHLEHEM

Ye nations all, on you I call, come hear this de-clar-a-tion,
and don't re-fuse this glorious news of Jesus and sal-va-tion.
To loy-al Jews came first the news of Christ the great
    Mes-si-ah,
as was fore-told by pro-phets old, I-sai-ah, Je-re-mi-ah.
His parents poor in earthly store, as weary they did wander
they found no bed to lay his head but in an ox's manger;
no royal things, as used by kings, were seen by those that
    found him,
but in the hay our Saviour lay with swaddling bands
    around him.
On that same night a glorious light to shepherds there
    appear-ed;
bright angels came in shining flame. They saw and greatly
    fear-ed.
The angels said, Be not afraid, although we much alarm
    you,
for we appear good news to bear, as we shall now inform
    you.

THE BABE OF BETHLEHEM

Ye nations all, on you I call,

come hear this de - clar - a - tion,

and don't re - fuse this glorious news

of Jesus and sal - va - tion.

To loy - al Jews came first the news

of Christ the great Mes - si - ah,

as was fore - told by pro - phets old,

I - sai - ah, Je - re - mi - ah.

The city's name is Bethlehem, in which God hath
    appointed,
this glorious morn a Saviour's born, for him God hath
    anointed.
By this you'll know if you will go to see this little stranger,
his lovely charms in Mary's arms, both lying in a manger.
Then with delight they took their flight and winged their
    way to glory,
while shepherds gazed and were amazed to hear this
    wond'rous story.
To Bethlehem they quickly came the glorious news to
    carry,
and in the stall they found them all; 'twas Joseph, the
    Babe, and Mary.
The shepherds then returned again to their own
    habitation;
with joy of heart they did depart, now they have found
    salvation.
O glory, they cry, to God on high who sent his son to save
    us!
This glorious morn a Saviour's born, his name it is Christ
    Jesus.

Back and forth Granny turned the pages of the old hymnal as
they went from song to song, and the sun of Old-Christmas Day
rose to sacred music.

Sarah and Tom had the table set, but breakfast waited until "The
Garden Hymn" was finished —

> *O that this dry and barren ground*
> *in springs of water may abound,*
> *a fruitful soil become,*
> *a fruitful soil become,*

the desert blossom as the rose
and Jesus conquer all his foes,
and make his people one,
and make his people one.

The two boys slept on. We moved to the table, and Tom bowed his head. "Thank thee, Lord, for providin' this bounty. Bless us and bind us. Amen."

Biscuits and coffee were steaming, and we ate without much talk. And soon the Weavers were wrapped to go. "Let 'em be," Tom had said when Little Rob tried to waken the boys.

"I don't aim to sleep. They can stay there, and I'll see they eat."

Granny took my hand. "I'm glad there's some folks gettin' interested in the old ways. This new generation don't know such things, but when they find the old songs and the old tales, they'll delight in 'em."

"There's no music," said Uncle Kel, "like the old music."

And they departed. Old Kel Weaver stepping carefully and picking his way with the two canes, last of all.

Jeems and I had our coats on.

"You fellers don't have to go."

"Got to be movin'. Just go with us."

"Feedin' and milkin' to do. Come back, and bring this man with ye. We didn't any more'n get started, Dick. I thought of a dozen more old tales while we eat breakfast."

James Turner and I got in the car and made the first wheel tracks in the clean white road.

THE END

 APPENDIX

ABBREVIATIONS

DASENT: "Popular Tales from the Norse," Sir George Webbe
Dasent. G. P. Putnam's Sons, New York, 1904.

ENG.: "English Fairy Tales," Joseph Jacobs. A. L. Burt Co., New
York. No date.

MORE ENG.: "More English Fairy Tales," Joseph Jacobs. G. P.
Putnam's Sons, New York and London. No date.

GRIMM, 1944: "Grimm's Fairy Tales," James Stern. Pantheon
Books, New York, 1944.

TYPE: Type number "The Types of the Folk Tale," Antti Arne and
Stith Thompson. Folklore Fellows Communications, no. 74.
Helsinki, 1928. Academia Scientiarum Fennica.

JOSEPH AND THE ANGEL

This tune is from the singing of Horton Barker of Saint Clair's Creek near Chilhowie, Virginia. The text is from several sources, oral and printed.

Shape-notes are widely used in the South, mostly in rural churches. This kind of music notation is simply an aid to sight singing. The *do* is movable but fixed in shape.

THE MUMMERS' PLAY

From: Marie Campbell's account of a Kentucky version, given in *The Journal of American Folk Lore*, vol. 51, no. 199 (Jan.-March, 1938). E. K. Chambers's *The English Folk Play*, Oxford at The Clarendon Press, 1933. "John Barleycorn," *One Hundred English Folk Songs*, edited by Cecil J. Sharp, Boston: Oliver Ditson Co., 1916. *Oral sources:* Walter Lam of Page County, Virginia, and Boyd Boiling of Wise County, Virginia. The version of the play as given here comes, in part, from actually performing a mummers' play with groups of boys at The White Top Folk Festival and at The Recreation Center in Charlottesville, Virginia. — I omitted the Doctor's long speech ("The Skoonkin Huntin'") to shorten the play.

GALLYMANDERS

From: R. M. Ward, Ben Hicks, Sarah Hicks, Nora Hicks, Anna Presnell, all of Wautauga County, North Carolina. Mrs. Carrington (Cora Clark) Mosby and her sister, Miss Alica Irvine Clark, of Lynchburg, Virginia. Parallels: "The Old Witch," More Eng., p. 101. "The Two Stepsisters," Dasent, p. 113. "Mother Holle," Grimm, 1944, p. 133. *Remarks:* The giving-out-of-breath is my own invention. "Seen a little gal . . ." came from the two ladies in Lynchburg. — If given a hint that they may do so, children delight in joining-in on both the repeated rigamoroles.

WICKED JOHN

From: Mrs. Jenning L. Yowell of Charlottesville, Virginia, and her daughter Alois. Peck Daniel of Bristol, Virginia. — The Devil's remark at the end has been used as a joke about Hitler. *Parallels:* Type 330 A. Zora Neal Hurston's "Mules and Men." Uncle Remus's "The Devil and The Blacksmith." Dasent, "The Master Smith," p. 105. Grimm, 1944, p. 367. *Remarks:* Mrs. Yowell called him "Wicked Jack." Her version started with the "Hillbilly" joke about the old, old man crying beside the road: "My daddy whipped me." "What for?" "For sassin' my granddaddy." — The Saint Peter (St. Patrick) business came from Peck Daniel. — Mrs. Yowell's second wish was on a shoehammer. — In the original John is an inebriate. — The fire-bush is *Cydonia Japonica* (Japan Quince), common to Southern yards.

MUTSMAG

From: Elijah Rasnik, John Addington, Mag Roberts Hopkins, Web Hubbard, Nancy Shores, Homer Addington (11 yrs.), James Taylor Adams, all of Wise County, Virginia. Cratis D. Williams of Boone, North Carolina. *Parallels:* Type 1119. "Mollie Whuppie," Eng. *Remarks:* Mr. Rasnik boomed out the old giant's voice most terrifyingly, and had Mutsmag answer him in tiny piping tones.

WHITEBEAR WHITTINGTON

From: Dicy Adams, Finley Adams, of Wise County. Bill Haga (15 yrs.) at Konnarock, Virginia. Martha Presnell, Mrs. Filmore Presnell, Nancy Ward, R. M. Ward, Mrs. Nora Hicks, Mr. and Mrs. Kel Harmon, all of Wautauga County, North Carolina. *Parallels:* Type 425, C. Dasent, "East of the Sun and West of the Moon," p. 22. Eng., p. 45. "Black Bull of Norroway," More Eng., p. 20. *Remarks:* The white bird is my alteration from Finley's crow. The naming of each of the three nuts is from Billy Haga. Dicy's title, "The Three Gold Nuts."

THE OUTLAW BOY

From: John Martin Kilgore of Wise County, Virginia. *Remarks:* Uncle Johnny insisted that Robin Hood "surely must have been an American." — Nora Hicks knows the Robin Hood ballad about the rescue of the two boys about to be hung.

SALLYRAYTUS

From: Kena Adams of Wise County, Virginia. — *Remarks:* Baking soda used to be called saleratus in pioneer times. (See Webster.) — Nearly all the elaboration here is my own, from telling the tale to smaller children. — The bear's remark about jumping is from a "fool Irishman" tale.

THE OLD SOW

From: R. M. Ward. *Remarks:* Mr. Ward had in addition, "Let my middlin's in." "O no, you'd middlin' me out." *(Sic!)* — Also, "Let my xxxx's in." "O no, you'd butt me out."

BOBTAIL AND THE DEVIL

From: James Taylor Adams, Gaines Kilgore, of Wise County. Ben Hall of Hayesville, North Carolina. G. M. Hogg (72 yrs.) of Blackey, Kentucky. Nancy Ward and Enoch Potter of Wautauga County. *Parallels:* Type 1030, 1036 Grimm, 1944, "Peasant and Devil," p. 767. *Remarks:* "That beats Bobtail . . ." seems to me a common byword throughout North Carolina and Virginia. — The hammer-throwing business was in a tale about Sampson and the Devil told by one of the sons of Polly Johnson of Wise County.

THE DEVIL AND THE FARMER'S WIFE

Tune from Horton Barker. Text edited by R. C.

OLD DRY FRYE

From: John Martin Kilgore, Gaines Kilgore, Palmer Boiling (15 yrs.), of Wise County. — Type 1537. A teacher at Pine Mountain School in Kentucky had a modern version of this tale with episodes in it concerning street cars, automobile, the doctor's office, etc.

CATSKINS

From: Mrs. Howard Ward, Shirley Johnson (12 yrs.), R. M. Ward, of Wautauga County. Dicy Adams, Mag Roberts Hopkins, of Wise County. Sally Middleton of Harlan County, Kentucky. *Parallels:* Type 510. "Catskin," More Eng., p. 204. See also J. Jacobs's notes to "Rushen Coatie," More Eng. tale LXXIII, p. 256, for all the "Cinderella" parallels, etc. *Remarks:* James Taylor Adams has a somewhat similar tale, "Seneca the Mush-Stick," which has the "broken ladle" business in it, as in the J. Jacob's "Catskin."

ASHPET

From: Mrs. Nancy Shores (now deceased) of Wise County. — There is a German (?) tale "Ashenputtle," but I have not been able to locate it as such in my copy of Grimm. — The magic washing of the pots is my own invention. Granny Shores had only the magic production of horse, dress, slippers, etc. — For "comb my head" the original had "crack three nits in my head."

MEAT LOVES SALT

From: Betty Lou Ramsey (7th grade, Wise, Virginia, 1945). *Remarks:* At first I had doubts about including this tale. Could the child, I asked myself, have heard Lamb's *Lear* read by her teacher? But how could she have combined it, on her own, with "Cap o' Rushes"? The magic of the white roses, the tower, the two older sisters being caught in "the briery bush" — none of this gave any hint of coming from print. I have found that there will be, amongst these natural oral tale-tellers, an occasional something that entered a *told* tale from schoolbooks. But I have not, in my setting down and re-telling of any tale, ever taken any clear case of elements coming from printed sources. This remarkable version of the ancient *Lear* story seems, in my judgment, to be entirely oral. I hope in the future to find other traces of this tale in Southwest Virginia and Eastern Kentucky. — Betty Lou could not (or would not for some reason) tell me from whom she learned this tale. I heard her tell it on three different occasions, and she tangled it up somewhat differently each time. I have merely straightened it out so that it would hang together. I added nothing. The "Duke of England" she also called the "Duke of Erlington." The old king made his crown, in Betty Lou's telling, out of briars.

SOAP

From: James Taylor Adams, Dicy Adams, R. M. Ward, Belle Kilgore, Emory L. Hamilton. — *Remarks:* This is "Stupid's Cries" in *More Eng.*, p. 211. — "Right there I had it . . ." is from another tale told by Mr. Ward, and once used by someone — I think I heard it in Kentucky — in this same *Soap* tale.

Skoonkin Huntin'

From: John Mason, Ray Higgins (16) of Salyersville, Kentucky. George Miniard, William Hardin Greer, John Greer, Jeanette Lewis. *Remarks:* This is the doctor's long speech in the English Mummers' Play. (See notes above.) It is quite common in our oral tradition. There is a parallel in Uncle Remus — "Gwine 'long one day, met Johnny Huby, axed him to grind nine yards of steel for me . . ." etc. This version is entirely my own compilation from these sources, and from reciting it many times myself.

Presentneed and Sam and Sooky

From: R. M. Ward, Nora Hicks, Kel Harmon — of Wautauga County, North Carolina. James Taylor Adams of Wise County, Virginia. *Parallels:* Type 1386, 1541, 1653, 1383. Grimm, 1944, p. 283, "Frederick and Katherine." *Remarks:* The name "Presnell Sneed" is my own invention. J. T. A. called him "Mr. Presentneed." In the originals the rogue's tongue is cut off with an old rusty pocketknife or a razor, or bitten off by the old woman. — Sam and Sooky is my own putting-together of another part of this same foolishwoman tale, which proved too much for one item. Title mine. In the originals the cards called her "lousy"; and the wheel called her a name — to which she answered, "Ain't never hoed a row of corn in all my life!" — Pointing up of the supper business is my own. Last episode entirely my own use of motif in the song "The Old Woman and The Peddler."

The Two Old Women's Bet

From: Maxine Caudell, Bonnie Creech, Thelma Campbell, all of Kentucky. Andersen's "The Emperor's New Clothes." — Type 1406.

The Two Lost Babes

From: R. M. Ward, Nora Hicks, Stanley Hicks, Miles A. Ward. — Type 327. This is our own "Hansel and Gretel."

The Twelve Days of Christmas

This tune is, in part, from the singing of Victoria Morris of Albermarle County, Virginia. Basically it is the "old" and fairly familiar English tune as given by Baring-Gould. Text edited by R. C.

Fair Day's Huntin'

From: John Greer of Laxon, North Carolina. I have included a few points from other tall hunting tales.

The Tall Cornstalk

From: "White Coon" Hubbard per James M. Hylton now of Bristol, Virginia. The "forty-foot well" is from Bert Tilton of Buckfield, Maine. — Gaines Kilgore heard me tell this tale once and the next time I saw him he said to me, "Richard, didn't you leave out part of that tale about the tall cornstalk?" Gaines had a twinkle in his eyes and I suspected he had been studyin' up something new. "Yes, I reckon I didn't get quite all of it in when I told it to you the other day. What was it I left out?" And Gaines, out of his own fun with this tale, told me how the corn that lined that well "got to fermentin' . . ."

OLD ROANEY

From: J. M. Kilgore, Gaines Kilgore, Charlie Wince Carter, all of Wise County, Virginia. *Remarks:* Munchausen, by substituting a nail for the ball, pinned a fox's tail to a tree and then slit its face and whipped it till it jumped out of its skin. — Mr. Ward took great delight in this tale, and told it delightfully but it came to him from the sources mentioned above.

OLD ONE-EYE

From: Ben Hall, Hayesville, North Carolina.

FROGGY WENT A-COURTIN'

Sources too many to remember. I have been enjoying this song for more than twenty years. Native oral versions of it abound. This is the usual type of tune for it. — The frog noises in this version came from John Bibb Tate of Marietta, Georgia, "son of Rev. John Ben Tate who was a Methodist minister in South Alabama."

THE GREEN GOURD

Remarks: This was one of Mr. Ward's best tales. I never heard anyone else tell it, nor have I located any parallel in any book. — I have elaborated a bit here, but only as hints and indications in the original led me, and after much telling of the tale to children. I never tell it quite the same twice, and after telling it I find it impossible to remember consciously what I should have included in putting it down. But one night when I told it to Harvey (7), Sylvia (6), and Laura (4), their parents, Darwin and Barbara Lambert, took it down as I told it. And thus several things were "caught" that enlivened the tale considerably from what I had already tried to write.

CHUNK O' MEAT

From: Baxter Presnell, Chester Farthing, Mac Farthing (9 yrs.), R. M. Ward, Anna Presnell, Nora Hicks, all of Wautauga County, North Carolina. J. L. Campbell of Dalton, Georgia. Alice Henderson (12 yrs.), Charles Caldwell (16), Ben Hall, all of Hayesville, North Carolina. Mary Ritchie of Fisty, Kentucky. *Parallels:* "Teeny Tiny," Eng., p. 65. "The Strange Visitor," Eng., p. 210. "The Golden Arm," Eng., p. 161. *Remarks:* On one of my first visits to Beech Creek, North Carolina, a small boy stopped me, put his foot on the running board, and looking me straight in the eye, asked, "You that man in here huntin' for old tales?" "Yes, that's me." "Did ye ever hear that 'un about the big toe?" "No, — " And the young 'un grabbed the top edge of the car door, as if I might go before he had finished, and without more ado, plunged into the tale. In the original a big toe is found in the garden, or cut from the big black booger's foot which is sticking out the end of a holler log in the bean patch, and this is what was cooked up for "meat in the beans." I substituted the chunk of meat because nearly everybody (except my informants, young and old!) objected to the big toe.

The Babe of Bethlehem

From: "The Southern Harmony," 1835. One bar is from the singing of Lloyd Fitzgerald of Waynesboro, Virginia, through John Powell, and as given in "Twelve Folk Hymns," ed. by Mr. Powell (J. Fischer & Bro.).